Redemption

Redemption

Melvin Sterne

LITERARY PRESS
LAMAR UNIVERSITY

ISBN: 978-1-942956-74-7
Library of Congress Control Number: 2019955384

Lamar University Literary Press
Beaumont, Texas

To my father - the finest and most honest man I have ever known.

Special Thanks:

No good writer is self-taught, and no good writer works in a vacuum. I don't claim to be a good writer, but I would have been a whole lot worse off if not for bunch of good people who patiently helped me along the way. In no special order these include Steven Quig, Marilyn Smith, David Bosworth, Richard Dunn, Pam Houston, Louis Owens, Clarence Major, Robert Olen Butler, Julianna Baggott, Mark Winegardner, Daniel Lazar, Mark Pearson, Mark Crimmins, and Caryn Voskuil.

Other fiction from Lamar University Literary Press

Robert Bonazzi, *Awakened by Surprise*
David Bowles, *Border Lore: Folktales and Legends of South Texas*
Chris Carmona, Rob Johnson, & Chuck Taylor, *The Beatest State in the Union*
Kevin K. Casey, *Four-Peace*
Terry Dalrymple, *Love Stories (Sort of)*
Gerald Duff, *Legends of Lost Man Marsh*
Britt Haraway, *Early Men*
Michael Howarth, *Fair Weather Ninjas*
Gretchen Johnson, *The Joy of Deception*
Christopher Linforth, *When You Find Us We Will Be Gone,*
Tom Mack & Andrew Geyer, *A Shared Voice*
Moumin Quazi, *Migratory Words*
Harold Raley, *Lost River Anthology*
Harold Raley, *Louisiana Rogue*
Jim Sanderson, *Trashy Behavior*
Jan Seale, *Appearances*
Melvin Sterne, *The Number You Have Reached*
Melvin Sterne, *The Shoeshine Boy*
John Wegner, *Love Is Not a Dirty Word*
Robert Wexelblatt, *The Artist Wears Rough Clothing*

Acknowledgments

I am grateful to the editors of the following publications where these stories were first published:

Best New Writing: "Redemption"
Eclectica: "Tiger Hunting"
Furrow: "Superstition"
Lalitamba: "Harijan"
Natural Bridge: "Sunyata"
Soundings Review: "Angel" and "Viraaga"
We Are Family (Math Paper Press, Singapore): "The Singer"

CONTENTS

11	Sunyata
30	Redemption
52	The Singer
63	Angel
74	Tiger Hunting
96	Viraaga
114	Superstition
131	Harijan

Sunyata

You have two irrational fears. The first is that you are going to spend the rest of your life alone and the second is that you are going to be eaten by an alligator. You are deathly afraid of alligators, though you weren't always that way. Once, in fact, you punched an alligator in the nose. Several times.

It is mid-afternoon and you just woke up from a nap. You were dreaming of one of those southern garden parties you attended as a boy, years ago, in Savannah, Georgia. There was a mob of people dressed to the nines (almost none of whom you knew), and long, linen covered tables with tons of food—chicken, watermelon, beans, ribs, roast, simmering pots of greens, and, of course, corn bread. It was a hot day in August, the grass thick and green, the air heavy and wet as only southern air can be. You were fourteen that summer, the awkward country cousin come to visit distant relatives in the big city. There were no other kids there your age. There were some just old enough for you to be odious and totally uncool to them. They made it clear that you weren't welcome to hang out with them, did their best to ditch you, and then made you promise, under dire threat, not to tell when you caught them smoking cigarettes and drinking stolen wine behind the boathouse.

Back at the party there was a gaggle of kids in the two-to-ten range, just young enough to be odious to you but not old enough to be trusted on their own. Guess who was assigned to watch over them? Yeah, you. The country cousin. Odd man out. Oh well.

You hadn't thought of that party in years. You hadn't paid much attention to it at the time. It was, at best, an inconvenient weekend in a forgettable summer. Your extended family squabbled constantly. Come to think about it—that was probably the reason your family was in Savannah. Some squabble or another. And that September, not long after the party, your folks abruptly quit the family business, sold their house, and moved to Arizona. There you had no squabbles with relatives. You lived in a little house made of stucco and kept a pet horned toad. There were no parties—you didn't have a garden to host one in even if you'd wanted to. And you hadn't thought about that party in Savannah since.

But there it was: the garden, the party, the dream, and you woke both curiously invigorated and vaguely disturbed, all at the same time. Funny what age and time will do to you. You yawned and stretched, sat up carefully in bed. *Carefully* because it wasn't your bed, but rather, a bunk to which you had been assigned, for you are attending a weekend retreat at Longquan Temple, a Buddhist monastery in the mountains west of Beijing. You sat up carefully to avoid bashing your head on the iron pipes supporting the top bunk—something you did the night before (and still sported the knot to prove it). It was late Saturday afternoon and you were alone in the room. Everyone else had gone to a chanting session—something you might have been interested in for five minutes, at most. But you had already done one chanting session, the whole two hours of it, and that was enough for one lifetime. Maybe two. That was Friday evening. This is Saturday and you learned your lesson. Earlier in the afternoon, your 'guide' directed you to the cafeteria, where the chanting session was held. You realized what was up and said, "No." Enough was enough. This was shaping up to be a lost weekend of memorable proportions, and maybe that was what reminded you of that garden party in Savannah, what was it—forty years ago?

You were at the monastery at the invitation of a friend and former co-worker, Xi. Xi emailed when you said you were visiting Beijing. She asked you if you wanted to spend the night at Longquan Temple. A simple question, but communication with Chinese was always an adventure. You envisioned a night of carnal love. There would be a long, incense-scented hallway lined with tiny cubicles with dark, carved teakwood furniture and ancient rock walls hung with exotic woven tapestries. The doors would be rough-hewn wood and the floor hand-cut stone, cool to the touch and bare, the furnishings simple and sparse, befitting a monastery. A table, two chairs, a single soft Tibetan yak-hair bed—no frame—only the mattress laid out in a corner. A brass lamp hung from the ceiling on a chain offered a slim finger of flame, while on the far wall, the light of the full moon poured like silver water through a slit window. If only life was as good as your imagination.

In reality this was not the sight-seeing, carnal vacation you envisioned, but rather, a kind of orientation intended to recruit new members into modern China's unique and curious Buddhist fold. You met on Friday afternoon and there had been a formal slow-hike up the

12

mountain. Two steps up, chant. Two steps up. Chant. After that there had been lectures, more chanting, a meditation session, and a vegetarian meal dished out by monks in a cafeteria. It had been a long day and rice porridge never tasted so good. But as for the carnal love affair—the participants were segregated at all times—the men and women standing separately, eating separately, and most decidedly, sleeping separately. You should have known. Really, the whole thing would have been a total disaster if not for two things. One was a Master named Junwen. The other was Ellen.

Ellen was the other American at the monastery. You don't know much about her, but you figured out pretty quick that she might be the reason you were there. She's a little taller than you, forty-something, but she's kept her girlish good looks. She has long, curly gold-blonde hair and cornflower blue eyes. She dresses like someone you'd expect to meet at a Buddhist retreat—hippie-style, with an embroidered white cotton blouse and a long, flowing blue cotton skirt. You didn't see her at the orientation on Friday, and you didn't notice her on the Saturday morning walk, either, though she must have been there. But she materialized out of the crowd of women to stand in the line right next to you on Saturday when you did your mid-morning meditation. You looked at her once, then looked away. But she was looking at you and smiling. You looked again just to make sure. You made eye contact. You smiled and she smiled, and there was nothing left to say. You knew. And you knew that she knew, even if you couldn't talk about it at the time. Before you'd said word one you were imagining telling your families how you met at this strange retreat.

The morning meditation was the best part of the day. You stood in a wide courtyard paved with gray flagstones. It might have been hot, but the courtyard was shaded by a half-dozen ancient ginkgo trees whose gray bark had been petted by monks for so many generations that the trunks were pockmarked with holes. The low sweeping branches were strung with lines of colorful, prayer flags in orange and blue and green and yellow and white and red, and when the breeze stirred they fluttered just like your heart when you watched Ellen walk. You stood through a lecture—sneaking peaks at Ellen (you did not yet know her name)—and then everyone formed a long snake-line and marched slowly and solemnly around the courtyard, circling a giant statue of a smiling Buddha, all the while chanting words in ancient Pali that nobody understood. The funny thing was, they had their chant, and you found yours, a kind of resonant, hummed, OM version of "Amazing Grace" that nicely complimented the nasal Chinese chanting of the ancient Indian words. And you walked around and around the courtyard, chanting, brushing through the low-hanging flags, and it was incredibly nice and peaceful, especially when you passed close by Ellen. Afterwards, the group leader explained that you had a break, a bit of quiet time to drink water and contemplate the morning's experience. Then you would meet for lunch at the cafeteria.

You had no trouble finding Ellen. She was right where you knew she'd be—right where you knew you'd be even if you weren't looking for her. She was sitting in the shade on the steps leading to the path to the Water Curtain Cave. She had somehow found a round, wide-brimmed straw hat. It suited her. She had picked some flowers along the way and slipped them into the hatband. They were yellow and purple, alternating. "Hello," you said.

"Hello," she replied.

You sat down beside her, close enough to talk but not so close as to crowd her. "What's a nice girl like you doing in a monastery like this?" you asked. It wasn't much of a line, but it was the best you could come up with on short notice.

She smiled. She was holding a small yellow flower. "Just thinking," she said. She twirled the flower between her index finger and her thumb.

"It's a nice place to think," you said.

She said nothing, and you sighed. Too many of your conversations with women started out bad—like this—and then petered out altogether. You suddenly didn't think you would like where this would end.

Ellen handed you the flower and then licked her index finger and made a simple sign on one of the stone steps at her feet. It looked like an upside down letter Y. You don't know much Chinese, but you'd been taking classes, and you thought it might be *ren,* which means person. But it also might be *huo,* which means fire. As you watched, she drew three sides of a box around it, one on each side and one over the top of it. Now, oddly enough, you knew that sign. *Shan.* It means a flash.

"Shan," you said.

Ellen looked at you, semi-incredulous. "I didn't know you knew Chinese," she said.

14

You blushed. "I don't. I just know a few words."

She smiled, a nice, child-like, I-know-a-secret smile. Then she licked her finger again and drew on the stone something that looked like a tree with one crooked branch and something that looked like a house.

You leaned over close to look. You could smell her perfume, and as you looked down, the wind blew a single strand of her hair lightly in the air and it brushed across your face. You thought you could die right then and there. "It looks like the little home I've always dreamed of," you said.

"Did you hit your head?" Ellen asked.

You thought about this for a minute, and then you remembered the knot on your forehead. "Yes," you said, touching the spot self-consciously. "I haven't slept in a bunk bed since I was a kid."

"You're from the south," she said. When you looked at her without answering she added, "I can tell by your accent."

"I am," you replied. "Sort of."

"Sort of?"

It's a story you hate retelling—the family, the squabbles, the moving, all that stuff. Instead of answering, you lick your finger and try your hand at Chinese calligraphy. You made two signs on the stone beneath what Ellen had written. One looks kind of like a box and one looks something like a man carrying a box. *Lishi*. It means, history. The weight of all we carry around. It was the second time you had thought that word on this weekend.

Now it was her turn to lean over and look at the marks. You were already embarrassed because your handwriting—even in English—is terrible. You can't imagine how ghastly your Chinese calligraphy is. The Chinese are so precise and the marks so complicated. You hoped you haven't written anything dirty or insulting. You were pretty sure you got it right because every day when you go to your office, the sign on the hallway door says *History* in Chinese. You teach literature, but your office, for some obscure reason, is stashed in the History Department. It makes life interesting.

Ellen—she has still not told you her name—squinted at the signs on the stone. "Prisoner?" she asked.

You think about this. It's one of the things you love about Chinese, and you love about Buddhism. Everything works in metaphors. Prisoner and history can be pretty closely related, if you look at them right. Before you could correct her she looked up and smiled and said, "I'm Ellen. From Savannah."

"Savannah?" you said.

"Ellen," she said again, "*from* Savannah."

"I see," you said. "I used to live near Savannah. But we moved when I was fourteen."

Ellen leaned down so close your heads almost touched. You tried to inhale quietly so that she would not notice, but you wanted to take in her scent and hold it like that for the rest of your life. What was it they said—pheromones? The sub-atomic and sub-conscious aroma by which lovers recognize one another? Ellen smelled faintly like jasmine incense and something else. Tea, maybe, or some kind of fresh mountain flower.

Next to your inelegant *lishi* she made two complicated square signs that looked, for all the world, like blueprints for a couple of houses. "*Yuanquan*," she said. And with kind of a triumphant smile she added, "Circle."

"I'm impressed," you said. "I would have never guessed you knew Chinese."

"What were you doing in Savannah?" she asked, not looking up. She laid the yellow flower down by your writing.

"Being a kid," you said, "but you didn't answer my question."

"What question was that?"

"What's a nice girl like you doing at a monastery like this?"

She stabbed her fingers at the signs on the stone. "Looking for answers, I guess." After a while she said, "And you?"

You thought about this. You were—are—also looking for answers. You always have been. It's what people hate about you. So serious all the time. You didn't want to tell Ellen this. But what was the alternative? You thought about telling Ellen about Xi and your unrealistic sexual fantasies, but then you thought that might not be such a good idea, either.

But when Ellen finally looked up, she looked at you with eyes so full of life and love and compassion that you wondered if she already knew. After all, it's possible that she saw you and Xi together, even if you had only talked briefly, and only a few times since you'd arrived. She might have asked Xi about you. What would Xi have said? That you were a friend, a former colleague, a professor at a Chinese university? That couldn't be bad, could it? But when you looked Ellen

16

in the eye you would have told her anything—even the truth. She was that kind of person. You could just look at her and tell.

Buddhists are supposed to tell the truth. You know this. It's the fourth of the Five Principles of Panchsheel. Even Xi didn't understand how you, an American, could be a Buddhist. Over here, everybody assumes that if you're a westerner, you're Christian. You eat with a fork, you wear shoes in the house, and you go to church on Sunday. But you're a Buddhist, have been for a long time, and find the simple, self-taught, stripped-down version of Buddhism that you acquired in America preferable to the highly-structured, complicated, rigidly-organized religion that is Buddhism in the East. You are most certainly *not* here because you are curious about their kind of Buddhism. You found the answer to that question a long time ago. What, then, were you searching for? More questions? "I'm here by accident," you said, but it came out lame. You told the truth and it came out sounding like a lie—the kind of inept excuse somebody makes up when they're caught doing something really stupid like cheating on their spouse.

You looked at Ellen. She was not looking at you, but rather, up the trail towards the Water Curtain Cave. She's leaving, you thought. And then you wished that it wasn't true. You sighed. What difference would it make? For all you knew, Ellen was happily married with a rich husband and five good-looking and above-average kids. That would be your luck, wouldn't it? What is it they say? *All the good ones are taken?* And you wouldn't want to come between a woman and her family, would you? On a Buddhist retreat? At a monastery? Would you? Could you? When you thought about it, you know that you couldn't. You know how it feels. And when Ellen turned and looked at you again—those eyes—you knew that you could, and would. You'd do it with her in a second. Right there on the trail if she asked.

But Ellen looked more sad than seductive. "Nothing happens by accident," she said, and then she stood up, looked back at the monastery, and then up the trail. "Have you been to the Water Curtain Cave?" she asked.

"No," you said, even though you were there last night with Junwen.

You met Junwen last night at the work party. Only in China could monks host a work party, right? It was supposed to be your contribution for room and board, even though you brought money and expected to pay for your keep. Instead you spent three hours filling plastic bags with sand and then helped carry the bags from where they dug the sand to a site where monks were busy putting up another building. It was the only time in your stay that everyone worked together, men and women, and there was no segregation. Xi was there, and she pointed you out to one of the Masters, Junwen. He was pouring over blueprints for the building and giving orders to the monks. The work was very orderly, even if primitive looking. Monks mixed cement by hand, shaped stones with hammers and chisels. But they seemed happy in their work, and Junwen competent at giving instructions, pointing this way and that, looking incongruous in his saffron-colored robes while wearing steel-toed boots and a bright yellow hard hat. Welcome to the 21st century, you thought.

Xi bowed as Junwen walked by and said, "Master, I would like to introduce you to Professor Steve. He is a teacher in Shanghai. He is from America."

Junwen turned on a dime and stopped, took you in at a glance. He was about your height, five nine or so, but younger, early thirties, perhaps, and slender. His skin was dark for a Chinese person, and he was shaved bald under his hard hat. He tucked the hat under his arm when he bowed to you and said, in perfect English, "Welcome to Longquan. We don't often have Americans as our guests. Are you curious about Buddhism?"

You told him that you were already a Buddhist, that you went for refuge in the Dharma in 1998.

When you said that he raised his eyebrows in a kind of child-like delight, and a smile spread across his face. "Will you join me for tea?" he asked.

Tea with a Buddhist Master was much preferable to passing bags of sand in a bucket brigade, so you said, "Of course," and followed him down the path and into a quiet hall that you presumed must house the resident monks. And in a small room (strikingly like that about which you fantasized), Junwen poured green tea into two tiny black, clay cups and sat cross-legged on the carpeted floor opposite the table from you. The tea was divine.

"How does an American become a Buddhist?" Junwen asked.

You suspected this was a trick question. He must have met American Buddhists before. You replied, "The same, I suppose, as you

18

did." You immediately bit your tongue and wished that you had not come across so defensive, or worse, arrogant.

But if he took offense, Junwen showed no sign. Rather, he poured your cup full again and continued. "I was just a boy when I started on this path. Really, it is all I have known all my life. This was in Sichuan Province. It is mountainous there, and we were very poor. There was a government school, but even though the fees were small, my family could not well afford them. I had a younger brother and an older brother. My parents wanted my older brother to quit school and go to work to support my brother and me in our studies. That is the way of things there. The older brother has the responsibility. My younger brother, especially, was very bright and eager at his studies. But my older brother, too, had dreams. He wanted to be an engineer. I knew then that I was destined to be a monk, so I insisted to my parents that I would be the one to leave school, promising to study in the monastery and send home what money I could so that my brothers could stay in school. They argued with me for a while but eventually gave in. I left home at ten and I have never returned."

"So you were born a Buddhist?" you asked.

"Yes, you could say that. But I was never satisfied with just being Buddhist. I wanted to help others in a deeper, more profound way. This was evidenced early in my studies, and the monastery sent me on to college. There I earned a BS and a Master's Degree in Civil Engineering. Later on, I earned my PhD in Buddhist studies at the Buddhist Academy of China, in Beijing. Funny," he said, "I became the engineer, and my older brother became a truck driver."

This surprised you—that Junwen could be both a monk and an engineer. Still, you find Buddhism more interesting than Civil Engineering. The world is full of engineers. "I didn't know you could get a PhD in Buddhist Studies," you said.

"Yes," Junwen continued, sipping his tea. "You must if someday you will become Abbott of a monastery. "But you haven't really answered my question. How did you become a Buddhist?"

This was the first time that weekend that you thought about the Chinese word, *lishi*. You did not say the word out loud, or write it on stone with your finger, but you thought about it. History. It is a question that has long bothered you—this business about history—because it is so closely tied to the notion of reality, which is itself a question central to Buddhism (or any other theology). If reality is based on perception, and might even be an illusion, then history is at best *the flawed perception of a past imperfect perception*, and at worst *the flawed perception of a past complete illusion*. There is no solace in serious questions like that, but you ask them anyway. Always have. But mostly to yourself because they make other people uncomfortable. You even practice making up examples that you offer as explanations in fantasy debates. For instance, there are many people who see you regularly on campus and, because you have an office in the History Department, will swear in court that you are a history professor, will take your position about historical events more seriously, make judgments about your likes and dislikes without ever having met you based solely on the observation that your office is in the History Department. But you teach English. So what is reality? Yours or theirs? Or neither? This is the thing that you hate about questions.

"It is a question," you said at last, thinking about all your other serious questions, "that would take as long to answer as all the events in my life from a moment a long time ago until now."

Junwen smiled, a broad, beaming, bright-eyed smile, even in the dim light of the room. "Well answered," he said. "In true Buddhist form. Would you like to go for a walk?"

The path to the Water Curtain Cave wound up the shoulder of a mountain that rose behind the temple. In some places (like where you would sit with Ellen), the path was of paved stone. In others it was carved from the living rock. It was already growing dark when you left, but you took neither lamp nor stick to make your way.

Junwen walked quickly and with a surprisingly light step. But then again, you are twenty years his senior. "I like this path," Junwen said. "I often walk here when I have things to think about. I have spent many nights alone on this mountain."

"I can see why," you said. The air was cleaner than in Beijing. Not alpine clean, mind you, but better by far than in the city. Still, the haze was heavy enough that you could not see the lights of Beijing, only a few miles to the east. Even the moon, almost full, leaked through the haze with a sickly yellow-orange hue. It was not unlike the colors of Master Junwen's saffron robes. You stopped beside a sign and you recognized one of the characters, *Shu*, which means, tree. It looked like two trees with a man standing in between them.

"This is the wedding grove," Junwen said.

It was not what you expected to find on a mountain behind a monastery.

Junwen took a deep, exaggerated breath. "Can you smell the cedars?"

You could.

"Many years ago, before even the first world war, this was a very popular place with the locals. In the springtime, on auspicious days, sometimes a thousand couples would come here for their weddings. On a single day. The trees here are very distinctive, with most being twins, that is, two trunks rising from a single root. The trees were very large and ancient, and the couples used to write their names on ribbons and tie them around the trees to signify that their love would stand forever, or at least, live long like the trees."

"It's a beautiful custom," you said. In the dark, you could see very little. Nothing beyond the first few trunks.

"During the hardships of the Cultural Revolution, the practice was condemned as superstition and many of the trees were cut down for firewood. It was a difficult time in many ways. But in recent years, people began to return. At first it was just a few old couples now and then; shy, nostalgic, returning to see if 'their tree' had survived. And then they came back with their children and grandchildren to show them what was left of the grove. Someone—nobody knows who—got the idea of replanting the grove, and now couples have started coming again for their weddings, and when they do, they plant new trees. Soon, the grove will thrive again—perhaps even better than before. Already the planted trees mature. It is one of the projects that Longquan supports. And the funny thing is, the trees that were planted have mostly grown twin with double trunks. Imagine that."

"Amazing," you said, and you meant it. You've long puzzled about things like that. It's one of the things that still confuse you about religion—this talk about miracles. It makes you almost as uncomfortable as history. Actually, you distrust that kind of thing. It's irrational. If there's any reason that you believe in God, it's the rationality of it all. Gravity. Mathematics. The laws of physics. Even the perfect principles of the Dharma. It's all a kind of perfect wheel. You like that. You like the order. There's always a logical explanation.

"How did you know," you said, "that you wanted to be a monk, even when you were so young?"

Junwen pointed up the mountain. "Do you see the path?"

Up ahead you could see the path clearly in places—the bare places—places where the steps were carved out the rock and glinted orange and black, orange and black, in the light of the sickly moon. Then it vanished, but even further ahead, in places, you could see the path, little bits of it here and there as it cut across the face of a cliff here, or passed through a gap in the wood there.

Junwen said no more. He turned and climbed the steps, disappearing into the shadows as you panted along after him.

The Water Curtain Cave had no water, no curtain, and wasn't even a cave, being, rather, a place carved out of living rock where the path cut across a naked cliff to another shoulder of the mountain. Junwen was standing at the entrance when you arrived. Turning back, you could see faint lights flickering at the temple complex below. You thought for a moment about Xi and you knew that she and your companions would be finishing work, cleaning up, and preparing for dinner.

"I suppose," you said, not waiting for Junwen to return to your question about why he became a monk, "that I was searching for something my whole life. A sense of belonging. A place—an intellectual space—where I could fit in."

"Fit in?" Junwen asked.

"Belong," you said. "I never felt like I belonged anywhere. Not in my church, not in my family, not in my own heart. I kept widening my circle trying to find something that would fit in beside me, something that could stand with me, comfort me. What I found, instead, was emptiness. *Sunyata*. And Buddhism was the only thing that explained that emptiness in a way that made sense."

"Made sense?" Junwen echoed your words.

"Yes," you said. "Buddhism is the only rational belief."

Junwen laughed. "If only Buddha could hear you now," he said. "Why is it that westerners insist on rationalizing everything?" He swept his hand towards the mountain the night sky as he spoke. "Even this."

"Why would you believe something that wasn't rational?" you countered.

"And why is it that you would only believe in that which you can fit neatly into your little intellectual circle?"

"I suppose," you said, "that that's the difference between East and West. But there was no East and there was no West when Buddha taught. There was only the Dharma. No monasteries, no temples, no teachers, only the truth. Life is suffering, but an end to suffering is possible. Suffering is caused by attachment, but when we let go of attachment, then we find an end to our pain."

"*Sunyata,*" Junwen said. "Emptiness. Is it really possible?"

"I'm sorry," you said, "I don't understand. I thought the whole point of Buddhism was that it *was* possible."

"Is it really possible to let go of attachment and retain the idea of rationality, both at the same time? What is rationality but an attachment to the outcome of an explanation? And why do we need rational explanations unless we are afraid of the emptiness that exists in the void of rational thought?" He looked at you as if he expected a reply. When you said nothing, he continued, "Do you know what motivates people? Fear. Fear of the unknown, fear of the emptiness, fear of the answers, fear of the lack of an answer. When we find that empty place we are seeking, what we find is that we are alone with our deepest fear. And people will go to any length to avoid that. People," he said, "are terrified at the thought of being alone." Junwen turned, then, and passed through the tunnel, pausing only for a moment on the other side, silhouetted against the rising moon. And then he was gone.

You rested for a while, noting only that the low flowering trees that smelled so sweet were, in fact, wild peach trees in bloom. It must be lovely in the daytime, you thought. Junwen was gone, and though you liked his cheery combativeness, you did not mind being alone. It was almost a relief.

"It smells like peaches," Ellen said, long before the trees came into view. The afternoon was hot and the air suddenly heavy. The sky darkened to the east, and you heard the rumble of thunder in the distance. You thought of the sign, *shan,* the upside down Y in the box looks like a man under a shelter. And sure enough, by the time you reached the Water Curtain Cave, the rain began to fall, softly at first, the drops like music in the leaves, then harder, the pattering of symbols that would inevitably lead to the crash of thundering drums. It fell, then, suddenly, in violent, wind-driven sheets, and you sprinted the last few yards to the shelter but still got wet. Under the rock the rain splashed on your feet, and you and Ellen huddled together like children to keep warm. You have been married and divorced twice, loved a hundred different women in bed, but no body you have ever touched felt so perfect in your arms. You wished that it would rain forever. You had picked a peach blossom on the way and you slipped the hat off Ellen's head and placed the blossom in the hatband among the yellow and purple flowers. It was pretty there, and for some reason you kissed her on the cheek, even though you did not know if she was married with a perfect husband and five above-average children, or anything, really, about her, except that she looked like the woman you always dreamed of spending your life with, of building a little house with, the kind of woman you could wake up to every morning for the rest of your life and never once complain. You realized then that you had not told her, nor had she asked, your name.

"Thank you," she said, looking at the peach blossom in the hat band. But you wondered—hoped even—that she was thanking you for the kiss.

The rain poured down and when you looked up, the tunnel really was, if only for those few moments, a Water Curtain Cave. The water flowed down the bare face of the mountain and over the sides of the tunnel, and it was a living curtain, and certainly a cave, and it was beautiful in a way that you will never adequately describe to anyone: the play of the light, the crashing music of the water, the ozone-scent of lightning-seared, peach-blossom-flavored air. Ellen's jasmine-and-green-tea scent, her pheromones.

In the depths of your chest you began to hum a throaty OM version of "Amazing Grace" and Ellen looked at you with those eyes and smiled like it was her favorite song, and you were sure without asking that it was. And for five full minutes you sat there, side-by-side, and you said not a word, and the silence was more perfect than anything you could say. *Sunyata.* It was the emptiness of perfection that required nothing, and you wished that you could see Junwen again to tell him that emptiness and fullness were possible—both at the same time—and then you realized that you were not alone, that Ellen was beside you, and that the emptiness was in your mind, but the fullness in your heart. Was it possible to be empty and full at the same time?

The rain stopped, the cascade of water slowed to a trickle, and the sun burst through the clouds. Ellen stood and stretched and said, "We should head down for lunch." You found yourself holding her hand as you walked down the path. You don't even know how it happened. It was like you had been together your whole life and there were certain things that you did without noticing. How you stirred

24

your tea. Which sock you put on first. The way you brushed back a stray bang when you looked in a mirror the first thing every morning. The same bang, always, and brushed back the same way.

You told yourself it was for safety but you wished in your heart that you could do this for the rest of your life. And you let go of her hand when you reached the trailhead, and you stammered a lame good-bye when you reached the entry to the cafeteria, where already the men and women were taking seats—separately, of course—and you wanted to ask her to meet you again but you knew the same way that you found her the first time that there was no need for this. And you practically floated to your seat, and vegetables and rice never tasted so good. And then there was another work party, and the chanting session that you got out of by taking your fifty-five-year-old back to the room and the bunk for a nap. And then there was the dream, and you were certain that you dreamed about Savannah because she said she was Ellen from Savannah, but then again, you know there is some subconscious and irrational part of you that talks to you in your dreams, and you wonder if it was that simple, or if there was something more to it.

There was something else that happened at the party, something you had forgotten about for years until the dream.

There was an alligator.

You were walking back from the boathouse and there was an alligator on the bank beside the river. It was maybe four foot long. Not all that big as alligators go, but big enough. It could eat a small dog or a cat or a duck. A child, even. There was a chain link fence around the property, perhaps three feet high. For all you knew, the owners put it there just to keep alligators out of the yard. But this alligator looked like it was trying to climb the fence. It couldn't climb the fence, of course. Could it? But it had its front legs hooked into the wire, and its snout stuck up over the top of the fence, just a few inches, but still, over the top of the fence. It wasn't hurting anything, just sitting there, but perhaps you were angry—angry about the older kids chasing you away, angry about your family and the constant bickering, angry about the long ride to Savannah. Who knows? You were angry, you remembered that, and you stopped and looked at this alligator, and then you did something you never imagined even in your wildest dreams. You stopped in front of this alligator, and you reached over the fence, and you hit it, right on the end of the nose.

You hit the alligator right on the snout. You probably didn't hit it very hard. You felt bone and reptilian flesh, but it's not like you broke anything. The bone was too hard and the padding too thick for that. And you weren't all that big—not muscular at all—and you didn't

25

know how to throw a punch. You were only fourteen. But still you did it. You punched an alligator in the nose.

The alligator looked at you, its green eye and black, vertical slit showing, if possible, even more malice than usual. It wasn't backing down, but then, neither were you. For maybe the first time in your life something had changed, and you might back down from the older kids, and you might back down from the parents, but this was an alligator and you weren't by-God backing down. You were, for whatever reason, learning something about fearlessness. And so you hit it again. And again. And the third time you hit it you knew the alligator was going to try to grab your hand, but it didn't have much leverage, and though it tried to lunge, the movement wasn't very far or very effective. Still, you anticipated the jump and you steered your hand slightly beyond where you'd hit it before so that the gator was left snapping at air. It bit and it missed. And before you could hit it again there was a cry behind you and then a mass of adults running and shouting, and someone grabbed your fool shoulder and jerked you out of the way. And someone else was shouting to fetch a shotgun, but in the end, they settled for jabbing the gator through the chain link with a broomstick until it waddled back down to the river and slid out of sight under the algae and lily pads. And then it was gone, not even a ripple. You blinked, and it was a memory. History.

The adults all shouted at you and ruffled your hair and called you nine different kinds of an idiot, and if you'd stayed in Georgia, they would have kidded you about punching that gator for the rest of your life. But you didn't stay in Georgia. And until now, you hadn't thought about that gator in so long, you almost wonder if you made the whole thing up. You weren't afraid of gators then. Probably weren't afraid until somebody said you should be. Or maybe it wasn't until you saw how quickly it disappeared, and then you were left to wonder for the rest of your life, What lurked beneath the surface of the water? You were not afraid of alligators then, but now you are. They haunt your dreams. You have not swum in a river in years. That was at the party, and it really happened. And then, for no real reason—except, maybe, that this is a weekend for asking strange questions—you say, Or did it?

And then you remember one more thing. It wasn't long after you had moved to Arizona that you came in the house one Saturday afternoon and found your father reading a letter from the family back in Georgia. He shook his head and tsk-tsked and tossed the letter on the kitchen counter. "Remember punching that gator?" he asked. You must have.

"Well, apparently it killed a little kid last week. You remember? Back at the party? In Savannah? Apparently it managed to climb the fence."

"I didn't know that alligators could climb fences," your mother said. She was standing over the stove stirring something in a skillet.

"Well, apparently this one can. Could," your father said, correcting himself.

"Who was it, dear?" your mother asked.

Your father was looking at a ball game on TV. "What? Who? Oh, I don't know. Some kid named Ellen."

In the dream, Ellen was there, standing beside the fourteen-year-old version of you. She was dressed just like she was today, only she was all in shimmering white, even her hat. You were watching the children play, and there was one little girl who had taken off all her clothes and was toddling around the yard bare-assed naked, but nobody really cared. She was only two or three. And Ellen left your side and floated to the little girl and took the girl's face in her hands, and the two of them turned as one and looked at you, and you were struck by how much alike they looked, only the child had the baby fat cheeks. But she had the same blue eyes and the same blonde hair, and you said, "You are the most beautiful woman I have ever seen." And Ellen said to you, "You are a handsome man." And you wanted to say, I'm not handsome, and I'm not even a man. I'm only fourteen, I'm just a boy, but you were there, the adult you, standing behind and looking over your own shoulder, and you—the adult you—said, "I'm not good looking, but I have a good heart," and Ellen said, "I know." That was at the party, in your dream, and it did not happen, not in reality. There no way that Ellen, as you saw her today, was there. And then you woke up, and you have never in your whole life felt so alive, or so afraid.

You washed your face and went outside. You went to the path to the Water Curtain Cave, but Ellen was not there. You went to the courtyard with the thousand fluttering prayer flags, but Ellen was not there, either. You found a group of 'volunteers' passing bags of sand and you asked about Ellen, but nobody spoke English. You searched the cafeteria and the temple. You looked for her at dinner, and again, after dinner, you took a flashlight and climbed as far as the Wedding Grove where the ribbon-bedecked twin trees whispered their love in the moonlight. On the way down, you found something even more alarming than meeting Ellen again. You found the rock where you sat and talked. The flower that she had been twirling in her fingers was still there, and the rock in the path still had the marking that you made with your spit and your fingers. *Ren, huo, shan, lishi, yuanquan.* Person, fire, flash, history, circle. It was impossible, you knew that. But there it was. You clawed at the rock but you couldn't pry it loose. You went back to the temple, your heart pounding, but now you knew, as surely as you knew when you first saw her. You scanned the crowd at dinner but did not see her. You had no appetite. You were the first one up from the table. You lay in your bunk that night but you could not sleep. In the morning, when Xi took a taxi into town, you made up an excuse to stay on a few more hours. You wanted a little time to clear your head. To meditate. That was it. To meditate.

You asked in the office. You said, "I'm looking for my friend, Ellen."

"Ellen?" the woman at the reception desk replied.

"Ellen. The other American."

"What other American?"

"You know, the tall blond woman in the long dress."

The woman in the office was Chinese. Her skin was light, her hair cropped officiously short. She was professional and neat. She flipped through her register going back ten whole days. Then she looked at you with eyes like stones and said, "We rarely have foreign guests here. If she was here, we would have noticed." She offered an insincere smile and added, "Perhaps she came on her own, wandered in from town with a tour group or something."

"Perhaps," you said, to save face. You thought you were becoming too Chinese.

Outside you found Junwen walking with his blueprints. He stopped politely to listen to your story. You told him you had a long conversation with a woman—not just any woman—but someone special, someone you would like to meet again. You told him about your dream, and your family. You even told him that you punched an alligator. When you were done you were sure he thought you were crazy. But if so, he was too polite to say it out loud. Instead he shrugged his shoulders and said, "Sometimes there are no answers, only questions. What is reality? What is time? What is perception? Does it really matter? There are some things that, like I told you

Friday, cannot be rationally explained. They can only be seen and accepted for what they are."

"And what are they?" you asked.

"Illusions," he said. "Everything is an illusion. People, time, dreams, history, rationality. Even your *Sunyata*. They are all illusions."

When he was gone you found a motorcycle driver and he rode you down to the subway station on the edge of town. You took the train to Tiananmen Square. On the platform an old woman rushed to you. She was selling umbrellas. "It is pouring rain outside," she said. Her manner was urgent, her accent thick. You thought of the rain yesterday and without arguing, you purchased an umbrella for thirty yuan, three times what it was worth. When you climbed the steps to the street the sun was shining and you wanted to be angry but you laughed instead. What else could you do?

The next day, riding the train to Shanghai, you passed through miles and miles of peach orchards. The petals floated down like spring snow and you remembered the fragrance like it was yesterday. Only, it was yesterday, whatever that meant. Or the day before. You had a compartment all to yourself. It was boxy, with two bunk beds. You wondered what the Chinese sign for compartment looked like. If circle was boxy, then compartment, you think, must be round and empty.

Outside, the orchards go by in a blur of pink and white. You remember the way Ellen's hair touched your face. One single hair. You remember the long line of her finger drawing signs on the stone, the scent of her skin, the warm pressure of her cheek when you kissed it. She never asked your name but you think that she knew. She must have known. You will remember this day for the rest of your life. *Ren, huo, shan, lishi, yuanquan*. Person, fire, flash, history, circle. You think of Ellen. "Prison," she said. Your history. Your prison.

When people ask you what you learned on your weekend at Longquan Temple, you have a pat answer. Sunyata, you tell them. You learned about emptiness. Junwen, the Master, was wrong. It's no illusion. You have never felt anything more real.

Redemption

Your father died and you're not going to his funeral. You know this will piss your relatives off but you don't care because you hate them and they hate you, and about the only thing that would piss them off more than you going is you *not* going. So fuck 'em. And you hate funerals. And you haven't been to synagogue since you were sixteen and they know it. And your father—and they know this, too—he quit going to synagogue not long after you did. And the last thing he wanted was a funeral.

The fact that your father didn't want a funeral is beside the point. Your father hated funerals but he went to them all the time. He used to say he made more money at funerals than anyplace. He said, "I make more money at funerals than undertakers, forchristsakes. And I *hate* funerals. When I retire, I'll never go to another one—including mine. When people get married, they make all kinds of promises about buying houses. But lemme tell you, when they die—that's when they get sold for certain."

That was your father, the finest and most honest real-estate agent ever to play the game. His obituary said that. The obituary he specifically wrote in his will that he *didn't* want. You know this because you have a copy of the will. Your father, the consummate professional, made sure that his lawyer gave a signed copy of the will to every member of the family. Your old man knew his family and he knew exactly what would happen when he died. A shark frenzy. And already it's starting. So you have a copy of his will, too, and that must piss them off, as well. But the real gem—and what's surely driving them nuts—is this: he made you the *executor* of that will. Yes, you, the prodigal son. And you can smell the lawsuits fomenting all the way from here, and that might be the reason that they have the funeral and the obituary and the whole nine yards to begin with—just to spite you. Or him. Or both. Only you ask yourself the same question. Why *me*?

You smile to think of your father not being at his funeral. Not fully present, anyway. He could be stubborn. Like when you got out of prison and he wouldn't let you in the house, not even for a few nights while you got back on your feet. So you slept under a bridge instead, even though it would have been a parole violation if they'd caught you. And you went hungry and you washed up in the bathroom at a gas

30

station until you 'fessed up to your parole officer. You told the truth thinking he'd send you back to prison, but instead he put you in a halfway house and found you a job. A lesson in honesty? Maybe.

But your relatives know your history. And they have to think it's some kind of scam you cooked up—this executor business—even though you've walked the straight and narrow for twenty-five years, the bastards. A nastier, more deceitful, hypocritical, collection of vipers the world never saw gathered in one place. They only thing they can agree on is how much they don't like you. And the only difference between them and you, you think, is that they never got caught. Or they had better lawyers when they did.

So they're holding a funeral and probably texting their lawyers during the service, racing to be the first in line to sue. And you let them go ahead and have the service, you'll even pay for it out of the estate, just to keep them off your back. They won't expect that and you haven't told them yet, but you will. Even though you don't know why your father appointed you, of all people, executor, you know that's what he'd want you to do. He used to say, "Don't try to be reasonable with unreasonable people. Cut your losses and move on. You're either part o' the solution or part o' the problem." He was full of sage sayings, your father. The ultimate pragmatist. But the funny thing was, he meant them. And lived them.

So they're at the funeral and you're in the house, and you know they've already been in there, too, because there are already things missing. Some paintings. A *real* Persian rug. The grandfather clock. And there are empty places in the china cabinet where you know there must have been something, but you can't remember what. You have the will and the list, but the list only says what-he-had and who-gets-what. It doesn't say where these things are. Were. You know your relatives will accuse you of stealing these things—even the very things *they* stole. They're like that, your family.

There was so much cool stuff. Statuettes. A jeweled sword from Mysore, India. A table from Morocco. Two massive teakwood chairs from Laos. A samurai helmet from Japan. It was another benefit of being in the business, your father used to say. People would sell the house and then there would be these estate sales, and you'd never know what you'd find there. And so much of this stuff, your father used to say, people just gave him. A little thank you for all the extra work. A set of antique porcelain dolls from Russia. Aunt Selma always had her eye on them. A humidor from Cuba with an engraving of Fidel

Castro on the lid. Uncle Ed smokes cigars. You sniff the house. He's been here, too.

You look around and you half expect the old man to shuffle in from the game room, or stroll in from the kitchen with his apron on and a spatula in his hand. Mom should be out back in her garden. There's a newspaper folded over the arm of the couch and the old man's slippers are there on the floor. An empty glass that probably had tea. It's like he ran to the market and never came back.

You walk into the den and see that somebody pried loose the black marble from the fireplace. The vultures. You rack your brain and wonder who's building or remodeling and wants a nice fireplace.

Your father might have made his living off funerals, but he was no parasite. He was a legend in real estate—and in a place like New York, that's a tough title to land. He was so well-respected he turned away customers because he was too busy to take proper care of them. "The most honest man I ever knew." That's what people have been saying about him ever since they heard the news. You wonder how many of the agents he worked with are at *his* funeral telling your relatives *how sorry I am to hear* and, *call me if there's anything I can do*. Your father would be both honored and disgusted.

Your father is one of those rare people who changed an industry. He wasn't born a real estate agent. After he got out of the Army Air Corps, after World War II, he did a lot of things. He drove truck for a while. He poured concrete for the highway department. He worked in a flower shop for a few months once.

That was how he met your mom—your real mom—making a delivery to a wedding. Your mom was one of the bridesmaids. They had a short conversation about the flowers, the ceremony, a few people they knew in common. "So when you gettin' married?" your father asked. "I don't know," your future mom replied. "How about next Saturday?" he said.

After they married, your father quit the flower shop. He went to work in the family business. They sold restaurant supplies. He'd steered clear of it until then, but he must have needed the money. More likely they needed him. "A man's gotta do what a man's gotta do," he used to say. And sixteen years he worked for that pack of jackals. Right up to the day they told him to put your mom in a nuthouse and divorce her. "That would have been like shooting her," he said years later. But she took care of that herself.

Three things happened after that. First, he quit the family business. Then, he met your stepmom. After that, he started over in real estate. You know it wasn't easy 'cause he told you so. He was six months in school and another six without a paycheck. That couldn't have been any fun. So when he talked to you about starting over from scratch, maybe he knew what he was talking about.

He took the classes to get his license, but your old man didn't just *learn* the business. He could have done that like every other agent does. But that wasn't good enough for him. In the old days, property values were what they were. If a house down the block sold for six hundred G's then your house was worth six hundred G's too, or more. Maybe there was something in dollars per square foot to figure out, but other than that, a neighborhood was a neighborhood and a house was a house.

But your father, he changed all that. A brick house cost more than a wood frame and a penthouse flat was worth more than one on the second floor. There were a million things to think about if you thought about it, and your dad worked out a whole spreadsheet for that stuff. When your dad talked value, it made sense. He could list houses, and they'd sell for damn near to the penny what he said they'd sell for. And he sold nearly all of his own listings, too. Most realtors sell maybe half. But not your dad. And he taught this to other realtors for nothing. When everything went to computers, he even wrote a program to do it and gave it away for free.

That was the thing about your dad. He had all this success but it never went to his head. You'd see these realtors driving around in a new Benz every year, but your dad drove a Honda. They'd have six new cell phones gizmos, but your dad had only the one, and an old Nokia at that. He never wore a Rolex. His Timex worked just fine, *thank you very much*. Outside of a plain wedding band, he never wore jewelry. He wasn't much for designer clothes, either. "A waste o' good money," he'd say. His suits came from Sears or Penney's, and on sale at that. Even his house—this house, the one you're standing in—wasn't some fancy-assed place up in Westchester or some million-dollar walk-up with a view of Central Park. It's a quiet little place on a dead-end street in Inwood. Not much for show and a long ride from anywhere, but so what? Your father never wanted the limelight. "Say less than you know and show less than you have," he used to say.

You, on the other hand, were just the opposite. Your father worked twelve hour days for years but you liked working a few hours at night. Your father believed in hard work but you liked easy money. Your father once rear-ended a car that then left the scene of the accident. He called the cops and insisted that they write him a ticket for the accident. You thought he was nuts. But he wasn't nuts. He was just the most honest man on earth. "Nobody's gonna come back in six months and sue me," he said. "Who's a jury gonna believe? I called the cops on *myself*."

You, on the other hand, sold dope and got popped for it. A kilo of coke can get you life for a first offense. You got twenty years and were out in nine. In prison you got a nasty scar under your left eye and a tat on the inside of your left forearm that reads: REDEMPTION. A reminder every time you wash your hands. And when you think about all the shitty places you've lived since then, the little house in Inwood looks pretty damned good.

But pops didn't leave you the house—that's mom's and you're okay with that. The will spells things out to a T. You sell the house and the money goes in a trust to pay her upkeep. She's in a home now. Has been for the past year. You're to send flowers on her birthday, and anniversary, chocolates on Mother's Day, and make sure she has something nice for Christmas. There's a fund for that. She likes earth tones and birds. Wool itches her. No fake leather. All the rest of the stuff is itemized. Who gets what.

And you, Mr. Executor, Mr. Big-Shot, Hot-shot, Ex-shot Con, you get one thing, and one thing only. An old, brown, fake-leather Samsonite suitcase the old man said is up in the attic. Technically, it isn't even in the will. It was on a stickynote stapled to your copy like an afterthought. Hell, you didn't even know the old man had an attic, much less a beat-up old suitcase to put up there. And as you walk through the house you keep your eyes on the ceiling and wonder where the access hatch is because the note didn't say.

You find it in the linen closet in the hall. Even then you almost missed it. There's no light in the linen closet, and you have to slide the top shelf out to reach the opening. And then there's no ladder. How the hell do you get up? Shouldn't these things have, like, fold-down steps or something? You find an aluminum ladder out back in the shed and stumble into the house feeling like Michael Caine in *Sleuth*. All you need is the clown outfit.

And when you get up into the attic there's no light, but you have a little LED keychain flashlight and that works okay. There isn't a thing to see except a dusty little path of plywood strips nailed over the ceiling joists. The path follows the ductwork down to the east end of the house where you know it connects to the AC unit outside. And you walk all the way to the end and almost all the way back before you spy the suitcase. It's an old carry-on bag down at the west end of the house where there isn't any path. You tiptoe ever-so-carefully along the joists to where it sits, right next to an exhaust fan and almost hidden under a stack of squares of spare fiberglass insulation. The whole thing is covered with a layer of dust and looks like it hasn't been touched in years.

You pick it up, and it isn't heavy, though something shifts inside. Slides like a lump. You sigh and tiptoe back to the hatch and wonder how you'll get the damned thing down, but you do, and then you carry it into the kitchen, rinse the grime off your hands, and get a glass of icewater from the fridge. You drink the water and look at the suitcase.

The suitcase has a combination but the note didn't mention that. You try the latch and it's locked. You think about throwing the whole thing away, or giving it to Goodwill and letting them sort it out, but there must be some reason your father gave it to you. Your father was born on December 9th so you try 129 and nothing happens, and then 912 and nothing happens. You were born on July 10th so you try 710 and guess what? It opens. Inside is the biggest bundle of cash that you've ever seen.

You close the suitcase. You go to the front window and look outside, but there's nobody there. You double-check that the front door is locked and fasten the chain. Then you come back and open the suitcase again just to make sure. The money's still there. Stacks of hundred dollar bills wrapped in a clear plastic bag. You open the bag and take out of one of the bundles. You run your thumb down the edge like it was a deck of cards. It feels real enough. Each bundle is bound with a crisp paper band stamped in blue ink by the Chase Manhattan Bank: $10,000. There are thirty-five bundles and a smaller stack stuffed in a plain white envelope. You count forty-one more bills. That makes $354,100, and you wonder how the hell it got there. You look at the bills and they are not all new, but they're in pretty good shape. You read enough serial numbers to figure it's not counterfeit. The oldest bill you see is 1959 and the newest 1973. That's the year you got out of high school and a year after your dad quit the family business and went to real estate school. You can't think of any half-million dollar prizes the high school gave out that you forgot to pick up, so it wasn't that. You don't think the family gave dad a big bonus for quitting the business, either. And he never played the horses or the lottery. You wonder.

You take the suitcase out to your truck and you put it behind the seat. You get behind the wheel and you start the engine, and then you shut it off. You don't want to sit there, but you don't know where to go, either. You think about where you might go with a suitcase full of money, and you think you could go any goddamned place you want. Well, not really. Hell, forty years ago you know where you would have gone. You would have bought a yacht and sailed to Jamaica. Putted around the Caribbean with some babe in a bikini. But that was forty years ago, and babes in bikinis don't give you a second look today. And $354,100 ain't what it used to be, either.

You go to Starbucks. What the hell. There's this chick there you know, Susan. Sometimes you hang out. She wants to call it something else, but when she brings it up you say, "Look, we're just hanging out." Susan's not there but her friend, Marti, is. Marti doesn't like you but she pulls a mean 50-50 just like you like it. Marti's one of these New Age lesbian types. She hasn't told you this but it's practically written all over her, from the tats on her arms to the rings in her nipples you're not supposed to notice. You order your coffee and ask about Susan. Marti says Susan doesn't come on until four-thirty. You check your watch. Two-ten.

You drink your coffee and you never worried so much about your truck in your entire life. You never lock it. You never wash it. "Who'd steal a truck that looks like this?" you say when Susan asks you. "Who'd drive a truck that looks like this?" she replies. You think about buying another truck, a nice, shiny, new one with a big chrome toolbox in the back. And then you remember your old man. *Say less than you know, show less than you have.* You got that right, you think. You decide that the only one you can talk to about this is mom, but you go home first.

Home is a sixth-floor rent-controlled walk-up in Queens. You've been broken into three times in the past eighteen months. Today would be the day, you figure. You put half the cash under your mattress and the suitcase with the rest behind a case of toilet paper you keep under the sink in the bathroom.

It's an hour's drive to mom's place. You buy flowers on the way. Your step mom is in a home out by Stony Point. A good home. She's been there since she got out of the hospital, after the stroke. The grounds are manicured. She gets good food and lots of personal attention. First class. Your dad made sure of that. On a good day she can talk for hours. On a bad day she can talk for hours, but to people who aren't there. Sometimes they've been dead for years. You know she knows about pops because you called her, but you wonder how long she'll remember and how she's taking the news.

Fortunately, today is a good day. Unfortunately, she's not taking the news very well. Fortunately, none of the jackals have been by to harass her. Unfortunately, she tells you Aunt Selma and Uncle Ed are on their way. They're driving up after the funeral. You check your watch.

Mom is sitting in a wheelchair outside by the goldfish pond. They parked her in a spot where it's shady and cool. There's a turtle sunning himself on a rock in the middle of the pond. There's larches and meadowlarks flitting in and out, some sparrows splash in the shallow end. Mom's in a blue silk kimono, her favorite, a present from dad. She wears it all the time.

"How you doin', mom?" you say. You hand her the flowers.

She takes the flowers, inhales the scent, and smiles. "I thought I'd go first," she says. "Ed said it was quick."

It wasn't quick but there's no point in disappointing her. He was gasping on the sidewalk on Broadway, *In front of God and everybody*, he would have said. Ambulances, firetrucks, cops, the whole nine yards. You picture your dad telling them to *Give a man a little peace to die in, willya*? Only it hurt too bad to talk. Or so they say. Heart attacks.

"We're here for you, mom," you say. "*I'm* here for you," you add. The rest of them never liked her—"the goy bitch," they call her behind her back.

She takes your hand as if she's the one reassuring you. "I know."

"You know... do you know... you need to know that he left..."

She looks at you.

"You need to know that he left you pretty well-fixed. There's the house. He wants me to sell it. He got a price in mind. There's no mortgage. Prob'ly won't take long. There's insurance, too. He left you pretty well fixed, mom."

"I know," she says.

37

You know that she might know or she might not know, and there's no knowing what she might know tomorrow. You decide you're not going to ask her after all.

"He worked so hard," she says. "All his life. He was always working. What was he doing downtown? He was always worried. A child of the Depression," she says. "That's what it did, the Depression, you know. It worried people. We lost everything. Your family. My family. So we were always worried about having enough."

"Yeah," you say. And you know it's true. You remember your father talking about diversification. "Spread your risks," he'd say. And you wonder if that meant keeping some cash around just in case. But that didn't seem like him. He'd have the money in a safe deposit box. And there was some of that. And some bonds. IRAs. Stocks. A few Krugerands. But everything your dad did was above board. Everybody knew that. You can't picture him with a suitcase full of moolah. Hell, if he'd found it on the subway he'd have turned it in to lost and found.

"You gotta make your own way in this world, Bud," he'd say. "Ain't no such thing as a free lunch."

But your old man, he wasn't tight. He was careful, but he wasn't a skinflint. He always had a few bucks in his pocket. The doormen at the hotels all knew him from picking up clients from out-of-town. Hell, once in a while they'd even steer somebody his way, somebody from out-of-town looking to buy. Or some relative or another. And he'd treat them and their families just the same as anybody else. And come Christmas he'd hand out envelopes. The checkout girls at the grocery store. The postman. The cabbies. The appraisers. The building inspectors. The plumbers. The carpenters. Painters. Electricians. The bankers. The insurance people. Hell, everybody knew your old man. And he treated them all well. And if somebody was a few bucks light, your old man always had a spare bill in his wallet. You never thought to wonder where it came from. He'd wave his hand and say, "Catch me later" like it was no big deal. Maybe they would, maybe they wouldn't. He never minded. He said, "I never loaned a dollar I thought I'd get back. I don't even write it down. You know, ten bucks'll buy you a lot o' happiness, but only if you give it away."

"Is there anything you need?" you ask, and mom says, "A hat. I need my white hat."

She hasn't worn a white hat in as long as you can remember. You look at her and she says, "Tillie's confirmation is next Sunday."

38

Tillie's been dead ten years. And she was confirmed in, what, 1940?

"Okay, mom," you say. "I'll bring it Saturday."

The next morning you go to your father's office. He'd been retired for years but he still kept an office with the firm. He's the only salesman who ever made partner. You ask at the front desk and Sheila sends you to see Morris, the president. Morris says, "We missed you yesterday."

"I hate funerals," you say. He's staring at you, and what you feel is suspicion. Morris and your dad go way back. He knows about you. You show him the will and the executor bit, and you say you want to go through the files your dad's office. You have the keys, but you felt like you should ask first. Morris is tall and bald headed, with a wreath of hair like a Roman Emperor. He dyes it black. He looks like the vain type, the kind of man who'd go for wigs, but he doesn't go for wigs, just a little Grecian Formula. He's wearing the biggest, ugliest platinum watch you've ever seen. A Breitling. He follows you into your dad's office and sits down. He's making sure you don't take anything important but he doesn't want you to notice. He makes chit-chat so you won't feel like he's watching you while he's watching you.

"Your father hasn't listed a house in years," Morris says. "Most of his time he spent telling stories and working on spreadsheets for the young brokers. He didn't need the money."

That's for sure, you think.

You look in the files and see that he closed his last deal in 2012. Three years ago. And even then he wasn't looking for work. Things just came to him. It's like that when you have a reputation. *Reputation.* "Hard to get and easy to lose," the old man used to say. You wonder about that. Maybe the good reputations.

The files are organized by year and the sales by closing dates. All alike. The names are there, too, last name first, in crisp block letters, all caps, black ink, felt tip pen. Neat. You flip through the files and they get fatter as you go back in time. The 1998 file takes up a whole drawer in the file cabinet. Twenty-nine sales. That's a good year. But that was before the bubble busted. And two of those sales were commercial. One went for ten-point-one mil. A three-percent share of that is—you do the math in your head—about three hundred thou. Not bad. But it was also 1998. And there was a lawsuit, too. That file was thick. You don't have to open it to know your old man came out on top.

The files get thinner again starting about 1985. Then you get back to 1973. "Amazing," you say, and you take the first file out and sit down in his chair, at his desk. Morris is still watching you. "I was eighteen in '73. How old were you?"

Morris looks up at the ceiling. "I was still at Harvard," he says. "Working on my MBA."

In 1973 your father listed six houses and sold two. It's all there. You remember that once—maybe while you were in prison—but you remember that once he said something about being audited. The IRS. You remember that he was annoyed but not worried, and he never brought it up again. "You keep your records straight and you don't have to worry," he said. That was another of his sayings. "Get it in writing. Keep it in duplicate."

"I joined the firm in '79," Morris says. "Right about the time oil went through the roof."

You wonder how oil got on the roof and then you realize he's talking about the price of gasoline.

Morris takes out a cigarette and taps it on the desk. You shoot him a glance, and he doesn't light it. "Say, wasn't that about when your dad remarried?" he says.

"No, that was '70," you say.

"And how is . . .?"

"She's fine. She's taking it as well as she can."

"A fine woman," Morris says, and you wonder how he claims to know her if he can't remember her name.

"Can I take these home?" you ask, looking at the files.

Morris grits his teeth like John Wayne. His eyebrows shoot up. He wiggles in his chair and speaks slowly. "We keep all these files archived, you know, just-in-case."

"Just-in-case of what?" you ask. "This stuff's thirty years old."

"You know: lawsuits, property disputes, tax problems, things like that. You can never be too sure in this business. Why, we've been called to testify over things . . ." Morris scratched the side of his face and looked out the window. "Well, several times that I know of."

"But don't you have copies of your own?" you ask. "I mean, surely these aren't the only copies of this stuff. This is just dad's set. And there have to be records in the courthouse."

"I suppose there are," Morris says. "But . . . what's all this to you? I mean, what do you want with it?"

"Dad left some notes at home," you say, and right away you bite your tongue and wish you hadn't said it like that. "I mean, he was always talking about writing a book, you know, about real estate. Valuations and so forth."

"I see," Morris says. "So the old man was writing a book."

"Sort of," you say.

"But all that stuff was numbers and valuations," Morris says. "You don't need any of this for that. This is just legal copy."

"Yeah, but you know how the old man was," you say. "It's all anecdotal. It's full of stories about this house and that house. The one with the pool on the roof that he wouldn't list because he calculated that the weight of the water was more than the joists were built to support."

"I remember that one," Morris says. "That was right after I got here."

You remember that one, too, but it was 1977, not 1979.

"And when it collapsed there was a hell of a lawsuit. Didn't some kid get killed or something?"

Nobody got killed, either, but you don't say anything.

"He saved the firm on that one. Had to testify, too, if I remember."

"He did," you say, even though you know it never went to trial.

"Yeah, he's got all these stories in his computer, but they're all organized by name, there's no way I can sort it out. He had all that up here," you tap your temple. "Like this one," you say, pointing at the first house your father ever sold. "Visquel." And as you open the file a certified letter slides out and glides across the desk and practically into Morris' hands.

Morris holds the letter up and looks at it. "Visquel," he says. "I remember your dad talking about this. This was his first house, wasn't it?"

"It was," you say.

"Well I'll-be-damned," Morris says. "I heard about this, but I only half-way believed it."

"Believed what?" you say.

"This was the one where the house got sold and the buyer never took possession. Your old man had $5000 in earnest money on the house, but the deal never went through. It was cash money, too. But your old man wouldn't touch it. He put the money in a special account and sent a cashier's check to the seller, but the check came back, unopened. Here, lemme see that."

You hand the file to Morris and he studies it for a minute. "No, it wasn't earnest money," he says. "It was rent. The house was vacant—the owner had moved out—but the buyer paid for a month's rent to take possession early. Your dad was like that. He'd think of everything. But then something happened—a divorce or something—somebody died—lost his job—something. So the buyer never moved in. Anyway. Your dad had this money, and he couldn't contact the seller, and so he sent the check to the last known address. And when it came back undeliverable, he sent it back to the buyer. And it came back undeliverable, too. Your old man was something, you know that? Any other man would've kept the money and kept his mouth shut. But not your old man. He sent that money back by cashier's check. Say—I bet that money's *still* in the bank." Morris flipped through the file. "Ah ha!" He produced a blue passbook with a single entry. "Five thousand dollars." He looks at you. If suspicion was a spotlight you'd be out alone in it. "Did you know about this?"

You shake your head. "I heard the story," you say, "but I didn't know anything about a bank account."

Morris narrows his eyes.

"Keep it if you want it," you say. "I'm just interested in the names. I'd like to match the houses up to the stories."

Morris puts the bank book back in the file and hands it back to you. "That money reverted to the bank a long time ago," he says. "But you can take the files home if you want. "But bring 'em back when you're done, okay?"

"Of course," you say.

When you get home you find a certified letter in your box from Baruch and Bartoff, attorneys-at-law. You open it and read, *In the matter of . . .* and you crinkle the letter and throw it towards the garbage, but miss. You also have letters from two real estate agents. *I'm so sorry to hear,* they say. *If there's anything I can do . . .*

That night Susan lets herself in and finds you slaving over your computer. "Isn't the internet great?" you say. "You can find anything on the internet."

"Marti said you came by yesterday," she says.

"I'm looking up people who bought houses forty years ago."

"I called but you didn't answer."

"I can find everything about this transaction except one thing."

"I thought you might call me back."

"They got tax records, court filings, you-name-it, they got it."

"But you didn't."

"You called?" you say.

"I called."

"I didn't hear."

"I noticed. Why are you looking at houses?"

"I'm not looking at houses," you say. "I'm looking at houses that sold forty years ago."

"So you're going to go back in time to buy a house? That's one way to make a killing on the market. Got any coffee?"

"No," you say. "I'm not going back in time. I've got some Gloria Jeans in the freezer."

"I hate Gloria Jeans."

"It's on the way home."

"This is New York. Everything's on the way home." Susan goes into the kitchen and you go back to surfing. She comes out five minutes later wearing a bathrobe over what looks like nothing and carrying a coffee cup. "So what are you not finding?" she says.

You look up.

Susan is blonde and blue-eyed. She's a few years younger than you, but not much. She's curvy and nice. A smile that melts chocolate. Smart. Funny. She's got a kid at Columbia and an ex-husband in London. She paints in her spare time and plots how to get an MFA so people will take her more seriously.

"What?" you say.

"You weren't finding something."

You think about how you would explain this to Susan and you look at the long expanse of thigh sticking out from under the bathrobe. You decide not to explain.

"How are you holding up?" she says.

"I'm holding," you say, and she looks at you like she doesn't believe you. She's smart like that.

After you fuck her she says, "What the hell's up with your mattress, anyway?"

"Nothing you say."

She wiggles around and says, "It's lumpy."

"It's getting old," you say.

"So are you," she says.

Sunday morning Susan wants to turn your mattress but you hustle her out for brunch at the Astor. Afterwards, you dump her off at Starbucks and you go home. You put all the money back in the suitcase and hide the suitcase under the couch.

You sit down at your computer.

So there was a townhouse in the East Village. It was two stories, a middle-of-the-block unit, not something that would attract a lot of attention. And the man that owned it was named Visquel and he came from Caracas in 1967. He went to NYU and then he had a little deli named Pabellon on 10th close by Dry Dock Park. That's what the paperwork says. He bought this townhouse for a song—paid less than 100 Gs for it, and that was nothing, even then. It must have been falling down so bad the roaches were moving out, but something happened, and you picture this guy and somebody—his cousin, maybe, or a girlfriend, or whoever—and they remodel this place, fix it up. And then in 1972 he decides to give it up and go back to Caracas. That's the address in the file, anyway. Avenida Pabellon in Caracas. The only problem is, when you Google it, there's like six Avenida Pabellons in Caracas. And none of them have anybody remotely like a Manny Visquel living on them. But you've got a certified letter, and it wasn't delivered, and inside there might or might not be a cashier's check for $5000 USD.

And then there's the buyer. His name is Manolo Edwardo Morales and his address is in Patterson, New Jersey. And you've got a certified letter to him, too, also returned as undeliverable. Well, sure. He moved out. After all, he was supposed to buy this place in the East Village, right? And he did, only he never moved in. And he never got

44

his rent refund. But maybe that didn't mean anything to him because money didn't seem to be a problem for Mr. Morales. He bought the house for a million six. A million six for a house in the East Village, and he paid cash for it. No bank involved. It was a cash deal.

That's weird. It was weird enough that some college kid named Visquel bought it to begin with. You think, *You gotta sell a shit pile of rice and beans in a couple of years to buy a place in the village.* Even then.

It sounds like one of your father's bad jokes. You know the ones. Something like, "A man walks in to a bar and says, 'I wanna pay cash for a house . . .'"

And there's something else about the deal—your old man's the only broker. You go through the files for a dozen years, and you don't see another deal like it. Everything else he's either the listing agent or the buyer's agent, but on this one deal—his first and only first deal—your old man works both ends. Double the commish. Easy money.

So now you got a seller who vanished into South America and a buyer who evaporated into the thin air of Patterson, New Jersey. And then you notice that the buyer's Hispanic, too, and you wonder—but his taxes show he came from California. But before that? Who knows? It's like he didn't exist before 1969, either. And there's not much else to go on except for one small thing. An obit in the *Herald*. And the obit says that Manolo Edwardo Morales died exactly nineteen days before he walked into your dad's office and bought a house. And that's not very likely. Unless there were two Manolo Edwardo Moraleses in this world. And that's not very likely, either. And the more you read about Mr. Morales and Mr. Visquel, and the more you look at the deal, the weirder it looks, and you get a really, really bad headache.

You decide it's about time for Susan to drop in unexpectedly so you go down to Charlie's for a beer. You haven't been to Charlie's for a beer in twenty-five years, but for some totally irrational reason you expect that when you walk in the door you'll find a whole crowd of people you used to know, and they'll be waiting like they've been expecting you. You try to remember their names, and you can remember a few, but not so many as you'd like. And while you're remembering you remember that the last time you went to Charlie's for a beer it was to meet Natalie and her cousin—this guy from New Haven who wanted a kilo of coke.

Ah, Natalie. It had to be Natalie. No informant was going to sell you out—you were too good for that. But Natalie was the real deal, pure FBI, all 36-24-36 of her. In prison you liked to say that she carried a pair of forty-fives. She also had a gun and some handcuffs. That was always good for a laugh. Especially the handcuffs part. And when they arrested you, you asked if she'd at least kiss you on the cheek goodbye. She said, "You dope. I'd wash my hands twice if I shook hands with you."

At first they busted you for conspiracy. You asked your lawyer if that violated your right to free speech and he said, "Actually, no." You learned that free speech doesn't apply to planning to commit even hypothetical crimes. But then they found the coke, which you had hidden in your dishwasher so that if the cops ever busted you, all you had to do was hit WASH AND RINSE and your problems would dissolve before their very eyes. If only you had been home when they served the warrant. "You must plan for every contingency," your old man used to say.

They also found a Colt .45, which they called *aggravating circumstances*, meaning that they convinced the jury that you were a bad-assed homicidal gangster—a murder waiting for a place to happen. You told them you were just being practical because, after all, a kilo of coke was worth about forty grand, even then, and you only wanted to discourage thievery. Your lawyer buried his head in his hands when you said this. "You mean you can keep a gun in your glove compartment to protect your car, but you can't keep a gun in your night stand to protect your stash?" you asked him. "You dope," he replied. You thought about this on your way to jail, the verdict still ringing in your ears.

Two things happen while you're standing in front of Charlie's. First, Susan drives by coming from the direction of your apartment. She doesn't see you, and she looks pissed. Second, you remember that not one of those cocksuckers in Charlie's ever called you after you got busted and went to jail. Not one. Not ever. And they never visited you, either. And the ones you thought you cared about are probably all dead, in jail, or sober themselves. And you only want to see them because of all that big-shot talk years ago about waiting for your ship to come in. So now it came in. So what? And then you think about Natalie and you think maybe you should go home and check under the sofa, and maybe you should change the locks while you're at it. You can't be too careful these days.

You change the locks, and you hide the suitcase in the dishwasher. You never use it anyway. You don't even know if it works. You go outside, and then you come back in. You wonder if you can cut a trapdoor in your floor but that would just go the apartment below. No telling what they'd do with the money. You go back outside and walk around the block. What the hell was your father doing with a suitcase full of money?

You go back home and Google "unsolved bank robberies of 1973." The most interesting case is from Ontario where a robber blew himself up when he was shot by a police sniper. The robber is dead but you fantasize about another, mysterious man—a robber nobody knew existed. Sort of like the man on the grassy knoll in Dallas. Only there's no money missing. Almost every dollar was returned to the bank. You look up D.B. Cooper but that was 1971. And all twenty dollar bills. You think about calling the police and asking if they have any unsolved robberies, but then you think that if you contacted the police about unsolved robberies they'd probably just investigate you, right? That's all you need.

You think about Natalie again. You never slept with Natalie, but you were hoping.

Besides. Your father would never rob a bank. Would he?

Your phone rings and you don't answer it. Susan. You don't have to answer it to know.

In the morning you call your boss. His name is Steadman. You work for a company called Steadman's. He owns it. Mostly you do iron work, but sometimes you pour slabs. You've been known to nail a roof, too. You tell him you're not coming in this week. He figured as much. "How you holding up?" he asks, even though he thinks he knows.

"I'm fine," you reply. "I just need some time to get used to things."

"Old man left you a pile of cash?" he asks.

He's joking but your stomach zips so tight you feel the acid all the way up to your tonsils. "Yeah," you say. "A whole suitcase full of money." Steadman laughs and says to take care of yourself, and you say you will. He says, "Don't drink it all in one place." He knows you don't drink, either. It's his way of encouraging you. After you hang up you imagine him calling the hall for another Ironworker. But what the hell? You can afford a little time off.

You go to Gloria Jeans just to spite Susan, and while you're there you remember this book you read in high school. Some poor fisherman finds a diamond or a pearl or an emerald or something. You weren't the best student in high school, but it was something like that. Everybody he knows dies and then he throws the thing back. The moral is . . . You can't remember the moral, but you're sure there was one. There had to be. Why else would they have made you read it? Your old man used to say, "Every story has a moral."

You think, *This story has to have a moral*, but the problem is, you don't know what it is. And then you think, *He wants me to hide his dirty laundry*. You think this, and you know you just let the cat out of the bag, and it pisses you off, but you can't un-think it. And you think, *There must be something else—something I'm not getting*—and you get in your truck and you drive down to the village and there you get another surprise. You go to the block where the townhouse is supposed to be and there is no townhouse. There's a whole quarter of the block gone—a big building there with a Trader Joe's and a True Value Hardware and a Walgreen's Pharmacy and a bunch of other crap. You double park, and you look at this boxy building, and you sit there until a cop raps your truck with a nightstick and says, "Move it or lose it, pal."

You come home, and what's burned on the back of your eyelids is this little red neon sign from a window on the third floor of this place: PABELLON'S.

You have a certified letter in your box from a lawyer named Farber. You open it and read, *In the matter of* . . . You crinkle that one up and throw it at the garbage can and miss.

Now you're looking up commercial property in the East Village, and you find this place, and it was built in 1974 and it's owned by this company called—get this—Inversion MoPac. You don't have to Google them to know, but you Google them anyway and, sure enough, they're out of Caracas. Malls and developments in forty countries. Mostly in the Americas, but Europe, too. Spain. Italy. And Asia. Singapore. Hong Kong. KL. Shanghai. Taipei. Seoul.

"What the fuck?" you say, right about the time Susan is finding out that her key no longer works.

"What the fuck?" she's saying, but by the time you get the deadbolt open she's out of sight down the stairs. You stand in the hallway and listen to her clop clop clopping out of your life.

Now there are two scenarios here. The most likely reason somebody would pay two mil for a place that was worth, maybe a few hundred Gs was if they wanted to launder some money. And if it's some dead guy's money you're spending, so much the better. So maybe some two-bit coke runner from Venezuela wants to clean up his cash and go home. Maybe. But there's another thing, too, kind of like insider trading. What if you knew that somebody was interested in a piece of property? And the value was about to go up? That might make you buy in, too. Especially if it had somebody else's name on the deed. And what if it was both? That's kind of like striking out two batters with one pitch, isn't it? You wonder who bought the house at the tax auction—Visquel or your old man. It ought to be easy to find that out, but somehow, you're not sure it will be—or that you even want to know.

"Every problem's a puzzle," the old man used to say. "You gotta take your time. Study the situation. It's not a race. The pieces are there, all right, you just have consider it long enough until you see it right. Don't get distracted. Slow it down. You gotta see what details matter."

Your problem is you never had the patience. You played chess with the old man, and he beat you. You played mahjong, and he beat you. You played poker, and he beat you. And now you're mad 'cause it feels like he's beating you again. He left you *his* mess to clean up. A pile of cash from some shady deal.

But that ain't it. If he'd wanted to clean something up he'd have cleaned it up himself. He didn't need you for that. And then you think, *Maybe it's not so complicated. Maybe he just wanted to give me the money.* But he wouldn't have done that, either. Your old man was proud of you. It took a while, but he got there. "You're doin' okay," he'd say. "You got three squares, a roof over your head, and nobody lookin' for you for the wrong reason. What more do you want?"

And what do you want? What do you want that $354,100 can fix? Nothing you can think of. Sure, you got troubles, but nothin' you can't handle. You're still standing in the hallway when Susan clops back up the stairs. "Why can't you let me in?" she says. You open the door. "Not there," she says. She taps you on the breastbone. "In here."

"I'm trying," you say.

Susan is in the kitchen wokking chicken. You're sitting on the couch when it hits you. You can forgive the old man for making a shady deal. You can see how a deal like that might walk right in out of the cold. New agent, reputable firm. Sure, why not? They want help and you need a paycheck. You haven't had a paycheck in a year-and-a-half and nobody's in your corner cheering for you, except maybe mom, and what did she have? A no-good job and a bum hip.

Maybe this was your old man's way of saying he was no better than you. When the easy money came along, he took it. Of course he did. So you were no worse than him. You were the same, you know. Only you know the old man wouldn't do that, either. Same wouldn't have been

49

good enough for him. Your old man wasn't like anybody else, and he wouldn't have wanted you to be, either. And you remember him telling you, the day you got out of prison, that "everything that happens in this world is a challenge and an opportunity. You gottta choose which. And you ain't staying a night in this house, son, 'cause you gotta learn to make it in this world on your own. And God help you if you don't."

For a long time you thought the old man was a heartless bastard for putting you out on the street. No—you didn't think it. You knew it. But he wasn't a heartless bastard. Everybody who knew your old man knew what a good man he was. And you may never know how much money was in that bag when he got it, but you can bet that after that first year, when the dough started rollin' in, the old man never took another dime for himself. But he didn't give it all away, either, and you wonder about that. If he didn't want it . . . *And then it hits you.* The last piece of the puzzle. And now you know why. The old man was giving you a chance to do something bigger than him, better than him—something he couldn't do himself. And to you, of all people, the ex-con in the family, he offered the chance at redemption. You get the chance to be the person you want to be, the person he wanted you to be, the person you were born to be. Your old man gave you that.

And then you think, *No he didn't.* Your old man didn't give it to you any more than money could buy it. It ain't his to give and it ain't for sale. God can't hit you with it on the road to Damascus. Redemption. It's a puzzle you have to solve for yourself. That's what the old man gave you. He gave you the puzzle so you could find the answer. *And it only works if nobody ever knows.* You can turn the easy money down. You can do that now.

Susan comes in with a steaming plate of chicken on rice. It's fire-breathing, her specialty. More spice than chicken. Pepper. Onion. Garlic. Stuff she gets from this Chinese grocer over in College Point. Stuff you don't even know what it's called, but it tastes great.

"I know this is hard," she says. There's a touch of finality hovering over her words.

"No," you say, "It's not hard. It's not hard at all. What's hard is living like this . . ." you tap your breastbone. "Living like this with it all locked up inside."

She looks at you.

"I'm sorry I've been an asshole," you say. "I've had a lot on my mind. But I'm okay with it now."

For just a flash you think about Susan and her MFA. You could pay for it. You could do that. But you know she needs to find her own way, too. Partners, not dependents. It will mean more to her that way. She needs a hand, not a handout. "I been thinking," you say, "that you mean a lot more to me than somebody I hang out with." It doesn't even sound like your voice, like you talking. Is there something different about you? Is that possible? You wonder what that look in her eye means.

It's nearly Thanksgiving. It's already cold at night and the Santa's are ringing bells at the malls, in front of stores. They've got those little kettles on tripods. They take cash and they give it to charity. You imagine materializing out of a crowd and laying the suitcase under the kettle. You'll want to be careful—anonymous—someplace where there's no camera. Maybe it'll make the paper. People will talk. They'll wonder why. But you—you won't breathe a word. Nobody would believe you, anyway, but for the first time in forty years, you don't care what they believe.

Yeah, the next year will be something. The relatives will bitch. They might even sue. But so what? Troubles squarely met, you think. You can handle it. You know that for sure now. And for the rest of your life, when you look in the mirror, you'll see yourself for what you are—and for what you do—not as you used to be, and not for what you did. That's redemption. It's gonna cost you what? Three hundred thou? Nah, you think, it's priceless.

The Singer

Everybody on the block knows your old man. His real name is Lee Hai Seng but they all call him Sing-Sing. Sing-Sing the fruit seller. Sing-Sing singing in his little shop, riding his bike down Old Airport Road, trudging the steps up to his flat. He's sold durians and pomelos and apples and oranges and mangos and papaya and dragon fruit and bananas for so long most people can't imagine him doing anything else. But you know the truth, and he knows the truth, and there are few old-timers around who know the truth, even though you don't talk about it. Not openly.

It's your shop, now, technically. Pa signed it over to you a few years back when he retired, but you let your friend, Steven Liu, run it because Steve needed a job and you have a better job than selling durians. Even though Pa retired, he still comes around every day and lends a hand. And Steve, who complains about everything, doesn't complain about this because he knows and you know and Pa knows that the only thing that keeps the old man going, even after all these years, is having something to do.

You're an engineer. Structural. Best of all, your specialty is fixing things. Other people's mistakes. They screw it up and you fix it. Anybody can design a bridge or a building, but can you fix an existing bridge or building? While it's in use? Without making things worse? Yeah, that's you, and you like your job. And you have a good reputation, too. Very good. So good, in fact, that you've spent the last two weeks in Taipei talking to the Ministry of Transportation about a pedestrian bridge that joins two downtown skyscrapers.

In this case, there's nothing wrong with the bridge or the buildings. The design is fine. The problem is that the idiots who installed the bridge *welded* the connecting structure between the two buildings. Welded—as in, permanent. Inflexible. Stuck. They should have bolted it and allowed some play. Now the buildings are tied together; their weight, their stress. And when they move—and you'd better believe buildings move—but when they move, the load shifts.

The engineers didn't anticipate what happens when you bind two free-standing buildings. The structures aren't designed to handle the extra weight. The extra stress is aging the smaller (and older) of the two exponentially. It's killing it. It's going to fall down if you can't fix it.

And sooner than those idiots in the ministry believe. There are cracks in the floors. The foundations are settling. There are noises in the walls. The tenants whisper about ghosts but it's not ghosts. It's stress shifting in the steel. And there's more. The gears on the elevator guides are wearing out in an imbalanced pattern. That's a bad thing when your elevator warps. What's next? The pipes?

"Can you fix it?" they ask.

"I can," you say, even though you're not sure how. After all, steel doesn't levitate, and you have cut this thing loose in place—and over a busy thoroughfare, no less. Without dropping it. You think that there must be a way, and if there is, you're the man to find it. You look at the problem long enough, and one day you'll see the solution.

The engineers in the ministry don't believe it can be fixed, and don't believe you when say you can, but that's how you got your reputation, right? You do the impossible. Do it often enough and people come to expect it of you. And the pay is marvelous.

You got in from Changi Airport around ten PM and Ann, your wife, had dinner waiting on the table. Little Lisa sprawled on the couch with an i-pad and a textbook, headphones on. She's studying physics to the music of BigBang. She's playing it so loud you can hear it even though she's the one with the headphones on. You hate pop music but you're glad to see Lisa studying so you swallow the urge to tell her to turn it off. She was eleven when she looked at you, with perfect confidence in her eyes and said, "I want to be an astronaut." Somehow you believe that she will. And why not? Look at yourself if you doubt her.

You've just started on the fish soup when the phone rings. It's Pa. You wonder what he's doing up so late. He tells you that he came by earlier and nobody was home. "Left keys under mat. I want make sure you have."

"The keys?" you ask.

"To shop."

"Why did you leave the keys?" you ask.

The old man coughs into the telephone and, for no reason you can put your finger on, you remember a scene from your childhood. You were standing outside the door of the little fruit shop. It must have been soon after Pa opened it, and you were just a kid. It was hot, so it was afternoon, but not on a weekend. You are sure of that, but you don't know why. Yes—you do know why. You had an armful of books.

You must have just got out of school. You remember the shop and you thought it the coolest thing in the world that here was this place with all the fruit you could eat, and it was there for the taking, any time you wanted it. And when you reached for a mandarin orange your father slapped your hand and you dropped your books. "*Zhe shi yao mai de*," he said. That's to sell. Forty plus years in Singapore and he didn't speak a word of English. Not back then. He speaks a little now.

You were young and didn't understand, but your Pa wasn't young, even then. He was in his forties when you were born, but wiry and strong. You remember looking around the shop and looking up at him—big, given that you were a child. You think about him now, thin like paper, so thin it seems he can't even stand up straight, and he tires so easily, and he has no strength in his arms, and he coughs all the time, and he's shrunk at least three inches.

"I not well," he says." He coughs again. "I don't know . . ."

You drop the spoon in your soup. "Don't know what, Pa?"

"I don't know go work tomorrow." He pauses while you take this in. "I don't know if go again. It long trip. Feet hurt." Another pause. Now he's speaking in Chinese. "You know, you get to a certain age, and you don't know how you're going to feel in the morning, or what you will feel up to doing, or even . . . even if you will wake up at all."

"Is there something you're not telling me?" you ask.

"No," he says. "I just don't feel well and I don't think I'm going out tomorrow. I'm going to stay home and rest. I'll probably be fine, but you never know, and I wanted you to have the keys. I also left a note—the combination to the safe."

"I know the combination," you say. You've known the combination for years, but lately Pa forgets things like that. You don't remind him of this. You also don't remind him that you already have a set of keys.

"Not shop safe," he says. "House."

You get up and go to the door. Under the mat you find five keys neatly tucked inside a sealed envelope along with a blue sticky note with *-9-3-3-7-# penciled in snakey handwriting. Two of the keys are for the shop, and two are for his flat. One key looks like the key to his bicycle lock. You come back and listen, for a moment, to your father's wheezy breathing. He's ninety years old. He's had a pacemaker for ten years, hearing aids for twenty. He's been in the hospital three times since January. He's humming absentmindedly while he waits for you to come back and pick up the phone. You wonder when was the last time you heard him sing.

After you hang up you walk out on the balcony. You're on the 24th floor, the top—a corner unit. Esplanade and downtown are off to your right, East Coast Park, the stadium, the strait, are stretched out in front of you. It seems like a thousand ships are out on the water, the lights like their own constellation. Ann comes out and stands beside you on the balcony. She looks back at dinner, growing cold on the table. "Are you okay?" she asks.

You hated your father when you were young. Your father woke you up at four every morning. That was one reason to hate him. And you didn't have a mom. That was another. You have a vague memory of her, sometimes, like something painted on the ceiling of a tomb ten thousand years ago. Like something painted on the inside of your eyelids that you might see if you didn't have to close your eyes to see it. She left when you were small and you never quit blaming him, even though you don't actually know why she left.

And life with him was hard for a boy. He left the house at five to open up and pack the shelves with all the fruit that came in boxes during the night—bananas from the Philippines, mangos from India, durian from Malaysia, apples from New Zealand. There was the fresh fruit to unpack and the leftover fruit in the cooler, and it all had to be sorted and inspected. And the sidewalk needed sweeping and the drains cleaning, the floors mopped and the glass polished. Pa was a real drill sergeant when it came to polishing. And he didn't trust you to sort.

He went to work at five and you went with him. He inspected and weighed and you did the dirty work. And he wanted you to come after school and help in the afternoon when things got really busy. And he worked late—nine or ten every night—and even after he came home there was dinner to cook and clothes to wash and cleaning to do.

You never told your father that you refused to help him at work because your absence hurt him. People don't often think of hate as a good thing, but it fueled your education. It was easier to tell him that you had schoolwork. A report to write. A book to read. A test. A presentation. There was always something.

Sing-Sing never went to school, not that you ever heard about. But he could add long lists of numbers in his head and was never a digit off. He could convert kati to grams and kilograms, and pounds and ounces in his head, too, and back again. Inches to meters, Malaysian Ringgit to SGD. He knew the exchange for Australian dollars and Thai Baht. Chinese Yuan. Pounds. Dollars. Indonesian Rupiah. He could convert centigrade to Fahrenheit. All in his head. If you're good with math—and you are—you got that from Pa. You have that in common.

The first time you told Pa you couldn't work in the shop because you had schoolwork, he asked what you wanted to be. You thought about this for a minute and said, "I want to be an engineer." You had no idea what an engineer was. It just sounded cool.

Your father looked at you like you were one of the new residents in the development and asking for credit. He narrowed his eyes and sucked in his lower lip and then dismissed you with a wave of his hand. "Go," he said. And maybe it was because you skipped out on work that he came home with that woman—she-whose-name-you-would-not-say—the one you still feel angry about.

In retrospect, he must have known that you weren't in the library, at Franklin's house, working on a play in the auditorium. Your neighbors must have seen you at the mall, the movies, walking down the street with your friends. But if so, Pa never said. He went to work early, came home late, and there was always something in the fridge to eat, and (in time) the cooler at the shop filled up, and the display tables overflowed, and she-whose-name-you-would-not-say began to work at the shop with your father, and then he married her and brought her into your house.

Ann looks at you with genuine concern. She is your height, with curly blonde hair and green eyes. She's pretty, and smart, too. And nice. "What is it?" she asks. When you don't speak she takes you by the elbow and you turn and look at her. This is one of the things you love about Ann. There's something about you that she gets. She understands you deep down inside.

Ann is Australian and that didn't sit well with your Pa. He expected you to marry a nice Chinese girl, but what could he say? He didn't ask your permission. You didn't ask his.

You say to Ann, "Did I ever tell you that my dad was in prison?"

"Sing Sing?" she asks.

"Sing Sing," you say.

"I mean the prison, not the man."

You look at her and then it dawns on you. Sing Sing is the name of a famous prison. In America. "I mean my dad."

Ann's eyebrows crinkle. "This is a joke, right?"

"No. It was after the war, but before I was born. I suppose that's why he was so old when he got married."

Ann looks at you with those soft green eyes. It was her eyes you first fell in love with. You met in Israel. Ann was a student at the University of Canberra. You were in the first year of your National Service. You were studying artillery and tank tactics. You had gone to Israel for some live-fire practice. Ann was spending her summer working at an archaeological dig outside of Tel Aviv. There weren't many young blondes in Tel Aviv. Even fewer Chinese Singaporeans. You and your buddies were drinking at a club when she and her friends took the next table. Your buddies dared you to ask her to dance, so you walked up and said, "May I have this dance?" You danced all night, and when you made to leave she stopped you and said, "That was fun. Would like to do it again sometime?"

You weren't sure what to make of that. In Singapore, you meet through family or friends. This was neither. And girls sure as hell didn't ask boys out. But you knew right then that you wanted to see her again. And you did. *How did you know?* you wonder.

Ann is looking at you and you know she will wait like that all night if she has to. She's so patient. Just like when she waited for you to answer whether you wanted to see her again when she had to know that you did.

"Murder," you say, "but they reduced it to second degree when they convicted him." You see the tiniest furrow on Ann's forehead and you can tell she's thinking.

Most of your life you thought people called your father Sing-Sing because he sings all the time. He's eccentric that way. You never asked, but you remember him singing as he pumped that old Hercules bicycle to work with you swinging your legs from a home-made rack over the back tire. You remember him singing in the shop while you swept the sidewalk. Singing in the kitchen while you studied algebra in the main room of the little HDB flat at Old Airport Road. Sing-Sing. He sounded so happy. But was it something else?

"The story I heard was that he knifed a boy in a fight over a girl. This was after the war but before independence. The Malays put him in prison, but after independence the Malays repatriated him. The boy he killed was local. I heard he was pretty well-liked. Better liked than Pa. And the family was connected. Some say it was her boyfriend. I also heard it was her brother. Dad had a hard time of it. So I heard, anyway."

"Sometimes people change," Ann says. "I would have never known if you hadn't told me."

"Sometimes." You look out over the strait and think about the ships. "He stevedored on the docks when he got out. It's hard work. I think it was on the docks that he made the connections to open his shop. He met people from the boats. He told me once he lived for a while in an empty cargo container. To save money. I can't imagine what that was like."

Ann is looking back inside at Lisa and you turn and look with her. Lisa's on the phone. Some boy or another. There's a new one every week.

Ann turns to you and shrugs. "I come from a whole island of convicts, so if you think this shocks me . . ."

"It's not that," you say.

"Then what?"

"I was just thinking. Pa is about the toughest guy I ever knew. Not like a bar brawler—that's not what I mean. It's just that he was always so focused on what had to be done. He worked sixteen hour days until his heart gave out. Seven days a week. He worked like that after mom ran off. All through school. All I ever wanted was a few hours of his time, but if wanted to see him, it had to be at work. I just wanted him to be like everybody else's dad. And I just once wanted him once to tell me he loved me. I suppose that's why I got rebellious. That, and he married Meizhu."

Ann never met Meizhu. She showed up a few years after your mom ran off, after you pretended that school was more important than work. She was *tang shan*. A mainlander.

Your father was a mainlander, too, but he, at least, came over before the war. He came to live with some uncle or another, but the Japanese took the uncle out in a boat and fed him to the sharks. Orphaned, your Pa spent the war on the streets fending for himself. So far as you know he never went to school. He never learned English until he learned the few words he needs to convince *farangs* to buy pineapples. Suddenly you think that when you said you wanted to go to school instead of working, maybe that was why he let you go and never said a word about it.

Meizhu told you three different stories of how she got out of China and you never believed any of them. In the 1980's, young women didn't buy plane tickets by themselves and visas didn't grow on

58

trees. You were fifteen when she showed up. The first time you saw her she was chopping coconuts with a machete. You walked up to the shop and started peeling a mandarin and you thought for a minute she was going to whack your hand off. But the old man came out and told her, in Chinese, that you were his son. And when you realized that Meizhu didn't speak English, you never spoke a word of Chinese again. Not in her presence, anyway.

"You know," you say, "I went to work once and Pa had a big, bloody bandage on his hand. I asked, 'What happened?' 'Chop coconut,' he said. 'Cut hand.' It wasn't until a month later when the bandages came off that I realized he'd chopped a finger off."

"Jesus," Ann says.

"But here's the thing," you say. "He never went to the hospital."

She looks at you.

You shrug. "I mean, what was the hospital going to do? They couldn't sew it back on. Not back then. The old man patched it himself and went back to work. I tell you, he was tough. I once saw him pick up a crate of passion fruit and throw it across Old Airport Road. All the way over. In the air."

"Why?" Ann asked.

"Who knows?" you say. "He threw at some customer." But even as you say this you remember that it was about the time Meizhu ran off, and it wasn't just "some customer." It was a guy who had taken to hanging around a little too often. You don't have to be rocket scientist to figure that one out. How old were you then? You were already done with service and about to go away to the university.

That was another thing. You had a scholarship offer from NUS, but you'd met Ann in Israel. By then she was working on a Master's at Queensland. You applied and they scholarshipped you, so off you went. The next summer, when you came home, Meizhu was gone. Your father never said a word.

"The thing is," you say, but then you don't say. "The thing is…"

One of the things you love about Ann and hate about Ann is that she is direct when she talks. You are Chinese and you talk in circles; you speak in metaphors and inference. When something is on Ann's mind she'll tell you, straight up. If she thinks you're being a jerk she'll say, "Don't be a jerk." But she also knows how to hold her tongue. She's patient in ways you are only beginning to understand. And when you look back on your father, it's not him you remember as hot-tempered. It was you. He was the guarded one. He was the one who buried himself in work. He was the one who was singing all the time. Yet he was also the one who, according to local legend, plunged a knife into his rival's heart. That was in 1949, but there are still families on Old Airport Road who won't shop in his store.

But now when you think about your father, you think about something else. You wonder what it was like to be an orphan on the streets of Singapore during the occupation. Your father left China as a boy and then he was an orphan, and he'd had his heart broken three times. You met Ann and you've never had your heart broken. You think about the war and you wonder what it was like to go hungry, and while you've gone hungry (for a while, a long time ago when your father was first starting the shop), you realize that you never went hungry after the first year. And you never went without shoes, or pencils, or anything else you really needed. But you think back, and you can't remember a single time that your father bought anything for himself. And all those years, the old man singing. Sing-Sing, they called him, so he did. But which came first, the name or the music? Were they reminding him about his criminal past, or teasing him for his habit? Was he really that happy? Or did he just not want the world to know it had him down?

"You know," you say, "I remember this time when I was home from college, a few years after Meizhu ran off, and I was at the shop and some lady griped about his scales and my dad stood up and said, in his best Chinese, 'Madam, my scales are inspected by the ministry every three months.' He didn't get mad. He just said. And it wasn't long after that his was the first shop in the market to have an electronic scale. It was such a big deal that the other vendors came just to look at it."

Ann smiles.

"The thing is, Pa was the most honest man I ever met. He wouldn't short change a customer. If anything, he'd give them more than they paid for."

You think of your father working mornings, nights, all the housewives buying fruit for their families, and him, Sing Sing, coming home alone to a dinner of noodles served up in a Styrofoam box. You used to be mad at him because, in all the years since you grew up, he never gave you a birthday present, not a single card. But then again, you never gave him one, either.

"Your dad's a sweet guy," Ann says. "He worked his whole life for you."

She says this, and you know right away that she's right. Maybe you never thought it before. There were no presents. No cards. No cakes. No nothing. Your old man never said he loved you. Not once. But all

60

that stuff is just for show, anyway. Anybody can give a present. Anybody can say one thing and do another. Your old man might not have said he loved you, but he did something better. He showed you that he loved you. Even more important, he showed you how to live. And you've seen a lot of people who don't know that. If you made straight A's all the way through your master's degree, who taught you how to work like that?

Maybe that was what kept your old man going all those years. Maybe that was his gift to you. Maybe it was all he had. No mother, no father, no wife, no friends. Life is suffering. Keep going. If you get lonely, *sing*. You wonder how a man goes from murderer to something else, and you think: he didn't hear it in church, and he didn't read it in some book. It was in the long days and nights alone—at work, in the house. You think of the way he looked at you when you said you didn't want to work in the shop, when you said you were going to school in Australia, when you said you were going to marry Ann. If his company—or lack of it—meant something to you, you wonder what yours meant to him. Your whole life you hated your father for what he wasn't and never took the time to appreciate what he was.

You turn and look back inside at Lisa. She's off the phone now but jabbing away at her i-pad. Facebook, no doubt. Telling her friends about the boy who called, and what he said, and what they'll do this weekend at the mall. You've never denied her anything and you realize that her life—no, your life—has been pretty much defined by looking at what your father did and then doing the opposite. All your life you thought you were a rebel, but it dawns on you that now, at the end, with your father gone to bed and maybe dying in his sleep, but it's dawned on you that you are not the rebel that you thought you were. You're tied together, you and Pa, just like those buildings in Taipei, and the weight of it all has probably been crushing him for years, and you never stopped to look or listen. And the stress is killing both of you.

Ann probably saw this a long time ago, but she's never said anything about it. Either the time wasn't right, or she figured you'd figure it out on your own, eventually. You look at her. She's looking at you, and you wonder if in some way you've been like this to her, too. "I love you," you say, and the words are so foreign to her that you see a look of bewilderment come over her face. "I love you," you say again. Not, *Please remember to eat your lunch* or *Please take some good juice or tea.* None of those obtuse Chinese sayings that circle the point without touching it. "I love you," you say, and the words feel something like freedom.

Ann leans forward and kisses you but says nothing, and you know, even in the silence, that she loves you, too.

You think of your father sleeping, and you can almost see his thin chest rise and fall beneath the sheets. You've always known, and he's always known, that one day it will come to this. One day at the bus stop, one afternoon on the bench outside the shop, one night in the dark alone, his heart will stop. It might even come as a relief. There will be a photocopied notice taped by the elevator and a small wake. A few friends will show up to pay their respects. Memories are long and, as the old man once told you, "Reputations are easier to make than to change." He was talking about business then, but the point applies to life, too. He probably knew that, though in his typical way, he would never have said so directly.

"We should take dad to a breakfast buffet in the morning," you say, and Ann nods. "We should take him up to the Pan Pacific, or the Sheridan. We should take him someplace special, someplace he's never been, someplace he can't even imagine going." But even as you say this you picture the old man, eyes wide, looking around at what must seem, to him, like all the food in the world.

You don't know if he'll even be alive in the morning. You don't know if he'll feel like leaving the house. You're forty-three and your heart suddenly aches, and you wonder if this is how the end begins, a slow ache deep down in the chest. It's going to be a long night, you think. And then you laugh, and Ann looks at you puzzled. Even if you take Pa to the buffet, he'll look around like he's seen heaven. But he won't know what to make of omelets or crepes or fancy pastries. He'll load up his plate with noodles, as always. It's just his way.

Angel

I got out of jail in Petaluma right after chow on a hot morning in July. I'd been picked up driving somebody else's car a month earlier, but since my blood alcohol was almost four I didn't remember. Apparently I drove the car into a ditch and when the cops came I tried to hide—in plain sight—in an onion field. They arrested me and I woke up in the hospital a few days later shaking like a sheep shittin' pine cones. After I woke up, this Sheriff's deputy—I'll call him Bill—showed up one afternoon and escorted me out of the hospital and into jail. He was the same guy who let me out thirty days later and walked me across the street to the Rectory of St. Francis' Church and introduced me to Father Flanagan.

"You know," Bill said, in the cruiser on the way from the courthouse to jail, "you are one lucky bastard. You ought to be dead. You know that, right?"

I wasn't feeling any too steady, and I couldn't see how my situation translated into lucky. Dead might be okay, I thought. Dead didn't seem too bad.

But this Bill fellow took an interest in me—I don't know why—and he took to hanging around outside my cell every chance he'd get and talking shit to me. I figured he had too much time on his hands. He had a cushy job. He was close to retirement and he was bald and fat and walked with a limp. He had a bad hip, he said, so he didn't go on patrol much anymore. Mostly he took care of paperwork at the jail and ran errands.

Well, the person whose car I took didn't have a clear title to it himself, and one thing led to another, and he decided not to press charges. So I only got nailed for the DWI and that was my first offense in California. The regular judge was sick that day so I got a substitute; a skinny, prune-faced old bastard with a cheap black wig and a red birth mark under one eye. I could have plea-bargained the whole thing away if I'd agreed to go to treatment, but I didn't like the idea of folks messin' around with my head. So when he made the offer I thought about it for about two seconds and told him to go fuck himself. He said, "Have it your way, wise guy," and sentenced me to ninety-one days and court costs.

But on the morning of the thirtieth day, Sheriff Bill walked me across the street to the rectory and arranged for me to have a cot in the basement. I shook hands with Father Flanagan, who looked old enough to have studied the sacrament under Christ himself, and then the sheriff took me to my first AA meeting. I wasn't too keen on being there, but I wasn't too keen on jail, either. And while I might not be too smart, I was pretty sure there was a connection between me being let out and Sheriff Bill sitting me down in this little room in a portable building in the parking lot behind the church.

I don't remember much about it. Outside on the steps was a couple of beat-up old winos picking scabs and bumming cigarettes. Inside there was a bunch of business types in suits sitting around, and some ditsy teenager with green hair and a ring in her nose, and she said she was some sort of secretary even though she didn't look a day over sixteen. And she read some mumbo jumbo out of a notebook while I looked out the window at a row of California bluejays yakking it up on the power lines. Most of the people didn't look like alcoholics. They were pretty normal looking, if you asked me, and they talked about jobs and wives and houses and the usual shit people talk about. But at the end they always said how glad they were that they didn't drink anymore, and I thought that was pretty weird.

When they called on me I said that I didn't drink any more, but I didn't drink any less, either, and they all laughed, and that was all I could think of, so I looked at my shoes, and after a while they told me to "keep coming back." Then Sheriff Bill talked, and it dawned on me that he was there, not to keep an eye on me, but because he used to be a booze-hound himself. That was probably why he was sixty-something and about to retire still a beat cop. And when he talked, he talked about stuff I could identify with—like crashing cars and losing wives and houses, and kids who wanted nothing to do with him, and being fired off jobs. And he talked about straightening up, too, and the things he did to quit drinking, most of which had nothing at all to do with hooch, so far as I could tell.

Then they passed a basket and people put money and slips of paper into it, and a few minutes later the basket came around again with just the slips of paper. I took one. It was a list with names and phone numbers and meeting times, and a note typed at the bottom saying that the attendee was required to attend five meetings a week by the Sonoma County District Court. Someone had scrawled *Blinky* on the top where it said *name*, though who Blinky was, I never found out. After the meeting Sheriff Bill wrote his phone number on the back of a Sheriff's Department card and gave it to me, along with two quarters and a five-dollar bill. He told me to call him anytime as long as it was before I drank. Then he went back to work, and I went downstairs to my room.

The church had a few rooms in the basement they put out to charity cases like me, but at the time, I was the only one. The rooms probably used to belong to the priests, but there weren't many of them left, so they had plenty to spare. Mine had an old, narrow cot with a lumpy cotton mattress on a spring frame, a single wobbly wooden chair (gray with age), and a worn-out dresser missing the handles on the drawers. Even though I didn't have anything to put in it, I looked inside anyway. There was a Bible in the top drawer—no surprise there—and a cartoon pamphlet about God's forgiveness. There were some mouse turds in the bottom drawer. And that was it. The sum total of my life. A Bible, a cartoon, and some mouse turds. And damned if I could tell the difference between them.

The room was stuffy, it only had one little window up at ground level. I scooted the chair underneath it and climbed up and pried the window open and breathed in the fresh outside air. Hot and dry. I climbed down and took off my shoes and socks and stretched out on the cot and wondered what the hell I was going to do with the rest of my life. In a few minutes, I was asleep.

I dreamed about crabbing on a boat in Alaska. I worked on boats a chunk of my life, but I had only gone up to Alaska once—that was enough. I went as an engineer, not a deck hand. The skipper, Tony, was an old friend of mine from the navy. The trip was uneventful. The boat had just been overhauled and she ran fine. Other than a few leaking gaskets she was no trouble at all, and I spent a fair number of hours on deck launching crab pots with the crew and then hauling them back on board. That was the worst part and the main reason I never went back. The deck was colder than a witch's tit in a brass bra, and the boat flopped around on these thirty-foot swells like a tub toy. It was twenty-five below zero and the waves crashed over us, and ever-so-often we had to stop and beat the ice off the boat with aluminum bats so she wouldn't get top-heavy and capsize. The engine room was warm, what with all the equipment running and such, but the deck was a whole 'nother story.

But in the dream, Tony, the skipper, showed me the engine room, and the engine was racing and lights were flashing and alarms were whooping and I was struck stupid—I didn't know what to do. Then he left. He and the rest of the crew got in a lifeboat and took off. My job was to stay behind and save the boat. I didn't have a fucking clue. It was like I had never been on a boat before. While I was standing there the boat was sinking, and even though there shouldn't have been any portholes below the waterline, there were. There were portholes in the engine room on this dream boat. So I went to the window and looked outside. The boat was listing to one side, it was going under, and the water was clear, and the sunlight filtered down, and the bottom of the ocean was pale yellow sand, and on the sand I could see, perfectly, the shadow of an angel—the body and the wings. I ran to the other side of the boat to look up, but I couldn't see anything on the surface. Then water began pouring in, and I ran back to the other side and looked down, and I could still see the angel, wings fluttering like a butterfly, but that was all I could see, just the shadow. Then the engine began hammering, and the water was up to my knees, and then I woke up. Father Flanagan was knocking on my door to tell me it was suppertime. Weird.

And for the first few days that's how it went. The old priest came around every morning and woke me up for breakfast and invited me to mass. I ate breakfast and declined mass. At noon I went to the AA meeting. Sheriff Bill would be there and he would ask me *What's up?* and *How'r ya doin'?* and *Do you have a job yet?* And I would answer: Nothing's up, I'm fine, and, No, I do not have a job yet. Then in the afternoon I slept, though I did not dream about angels again. In the evening Father Flanagan came around and woke me up for supper, and afterwards I went to another AA meeting somewhere in town and then I walked around until late because I couldn't sleep and had nothing else to do. The church didn't offer lunch so I didn't eat but two meals a day. I kept the five bucks and the quarters, but I didn't spend them. I carried them in my pocket so it wouldn't feel empty. I also kept the paper with the phone numbers, but I hadn't thought about calling anyone.

On the fourth night, walking around after a meeting, I stopped in front of the Sporthaus Tavern and looked in the window at the folks playing pool or sitting at the bar watching the ballgame on TV. For twenty years that was my life. You go to work and make your money and you come home and spend it. It seemed like a good idea at the time. While I was standing there, my face practically mashed into the window, a couple of women pulled up in an old beater Ford truck. One of them was dark-haired and thin, kind of scraggly-looking, with a pockmarked face. The other one was blonde, short and a little bit pudgy, and she had a hole in her jeans right below the back pocket and her ass showed through. No panties. "Fourteen was the best year for me," she said as she walked by. "At fourteen I was hotter 'n jalapenos."

"I didn't know anything at fourteen," said the other. "I was just getting started."

"Fourteen kicked ass," the first one said.

They walked into the tavern and sauntered up to the bar, and a minute later a couple of cowboys sidled up alongside them and turned on the charm. I would've turned on the charm, too, if I'd had any to spare. But seeing as how I only had five dollars and fifty cents to my name and hadn't washed my clothes in a week, I prob'ly woulda had better luck trying to fly to the moon. But I did have five bucks, and that could get me a bottle of something. Hell, they sell hard liquor everywhere in California. Next door to the Sporthaus was a Bartell Drugs, and I could get a bottle of Jack there.

But outside the drugstore was a phone booth, and for some reason, instead of going in and buying the booze, I stopped and dug out Sheriff Bill's phone number. I dropped a quarter in the slot and dialed, and the phone rang. Then it picked up and a raspy voice said, "I'm not home right now, but . . . "

I hung up and stood for a little while, scratching my palms. It was hot. The sun was gone, but it wasn't full dark yet. There was little sliver of red on the horizon, and I knew that somewhere over the Pacific there was a ship and a crew and somebody was watching a big red ball of a sun going down. A little drop of sweat trickled past my eyebrow and burned in the corner of my eye. A roar of cheers rose from the bar and somebody laughed and shouted, "Yeah, baby!"

I took out the paper and looked down the list of names, and damned if any of them looked familiar. I decided I would call one more person—just one—and if somebody answered I would talk to them. If I got a machine, or if they wouldn't talk, then to hell with it, I'd go get drunk. So I dialed the first number that struck me and after a few rings a voice answered and a man said, "Hello."

Suddenly I felt stupid again. I didn't know what to say. My tongue tied and I stood there in this phone booth on the corner of Second and Main, and then the man said again, "Hello."

"Hello," I said.

"Hello, again," the man said. "Can I help you?"

"Yes," I said. "I don't know. I've never done this before, I mean, I feel kind of stupid here."

"I can see why," he said. "What do you want?"

"Well," I said, "I don't know. I don't think we've ever met. I got this number off a paper in a basket in an AA meeting. It wasn't even my paper, I just took it because it was my first meeting and I thought it was something they passed around for people to take. I actually thought it was like a coupon for a sandwich or something or maybe a discount for some clothes at a thrift store. I could use some clean clothes. I've been wearing these since I got out of jail. Almost a week now. You should be glad I'm calling from a payphone and you can't smell me."

"I'm sorry," the man said, "are you asking me for clothes?"

"No," I said. "I'm not asking you for anything. I just—I got these two quarters from Sheriff Bill and he told me to call before I drank, but he's not home, so I'm calling. I don't know what else to do. I don't know you. I don't know who you are or if we've ever met. I was just calling because I don't want to drink tonight."

"You're a few twigs shy of a bird's nest, aren't you?" the man said.

I laughed. "Yes," I said, "You could say that. You certainly could."

A semi lumbered down the road and slowed to a stop outside the tavern. The driver set the brakes with a sharp hiss and ran inside. He must have ordered a six-pack to go. The bartender went back in the cooler and came out with a paper sack. The man on the phone said something I couldn't hear. "I can't hear you," I said, "There's a truck right outside the phone booth. Can you hold on just a sec?"

The driver left some money on the bar, tipped his hat to the grungy girls, and came back out. On the sidewalk he pulled a beer from the bag and popped a top, and drained it in one long, cool pull. Then he crumpled the can and threw it on the tavern's roof. He climbed into the truck and drove away. When he was gone I said, "He's gone," and the man said, "Okay."

After a long pause he said, "Is a drink going to solve any of your problems?"

"No," I said. "Prob'ly not."

And then he asked me a strange question: "What is?"

"What is what?"

"What is going to solve your problems?"

I watched the moths circling around the orange bulb of a streetlight, and I had to admit I didn't know. "I don't know," I said. I'm forty fucking years old and I don't have a fucking clue."

"That's the first step," he said, "admitting that we're licked. Don't drink, and keep going to meetings. You'll figure it out."

"That's it?"

"For now," he said. "Go to bed sober tonight and you'll be one day closer to a better life. You think you can do that?"

"I guess so," I said. "I mean, I went to bed last night without drinking."

"You guess so?"

"Yeah," I said. "I can do that."

"So do you feel better now?"

"Yes. Yes I do."

"You didn't drink, did you?" he asked, and I said "No."

"Good," he said. "The hardest thing is not to pick up the first one. But if you can do that, you'll never drink again—even if you want to."

"But never is a long time," I said. "How can I say I'll never do anything again?"

"You don't have to," he said. "You don't have to do anything forever. Just ask yourself: Can I go to bed sober tonight?"

"I can do that," I said.

"That's all you ever have to do."

"Thank you," I said, and then after a while he asked me if there was anything else he could do. "No," I said. "I think I'll be all right now."

"Good night," he said, and he hung up.

After I got off the phone I walked into Bartells. I went to the magazine rack first, but they didn't have much: *GQ, Sports Illustrated, Maxim*, some romance rags, *Car and Driver*. Beyond it was the liquor aisle and I looked down the rows of bottles. Gibley's Gin. I used to drink that. Vodka, too. It's cheap. I had five bucks in my pocket, but for some reason I didn't want to drink. I wanted to walk down that aisle with my arms outstretched and touch every bottle. I felt bullet proof, like I'd been washed clean.

I walked back to the rectory with a bag tucked under my arm, and I sat down on my bed. I had a notebook, a pen, and a box of envelopes, but no stamps. I didn't have enough money for stamps. I took off my shoes and socks—they smelled pretty ripe by now—and I set them outside my door. Then I laid down and started to write. I wrote a letter to the man whose car I stole and promised to pay him back for the damages after I got a job. Then I wrote a letter to my ex-wife. I don't know why I wrote her; she'd probably be just as glad to hear I was being roasted by cannibals as living in some church basement, but I wrote anyway, and said I was sorry for being such an asshole. And I wrote a letter to my son saying I hoped he was well, and I understood if he didn't want to see me again, but that I hoped he would.

I was on a roll. I couldn't stop. I couldn't put down the pen. My back ached from writing lying down, so I took the chair outside and set it under the streetlight in the parking lot and wrote some more. I wrote letters to old friends whose addresses I didn't know. I wrote a letter to Tony, the crab boat skipper, but I didn't mention the dream. I wrote a letter to my mother, who was dead, and another one to my father, who was blind and living in some old-folks home outside of Tampa. There was a cloud of moths around the light, there must have been a thousand of them, and every now and then one would swoop down on me, hit me with a little wing dust. A police cruiser drove by slowly, turned around at the end of the block, and drove by again. I wrote until my legs went numb, then I got up and walked around until the feeling came back. I flapped my arms to keep warm. And then I wrote some more. The dew fell, and my paper got damp.

At dawn I went inside and took a shower. When Father Flanagan came by I asked if there was something I could do around the church to earn a few dollars. "Nobody will hire a bum like me," I said. "But if you'll give me a chance, just for a little while, a month at the outside, maybe I can find work." I said that if he could see his way to lend me a few bucks, I would buy some clothes at the thrift store, and I could wash the ones I had on. "It'll help me get a job," I said. After breakfast I did the dishes. I almost had to fight the old priest to let me. "Let me," I said. "It's the least I can do." And Flannigan gave me a few bucks, and damned if I didn't get a dishwashing job that night.

A few weeks later I was sitting in a meeting with Sheriff Bill when some old fart came in late and told the strangest story. Late one night a few weeks ago, he said, he was sitting in his kitchen with a bottle of Jim Beam and a .357 magnum. He was gonna get drunk and then blow his brains out. His wife had died awhile back, and he was getting up in years, and he was depressed, wasn't sure he wanted to go on anymore. So he wrote a note and sat down to get smashed so he could blow his brains out. He'd opened the bottle, and he got up to get some ice cubes. But some yahoo got ahold of his number and called him from a bar. The guy was about goofy, he said, but he called up instead of drinking and so he had talked to the man. For all I know, he said, the guy went ahead and drank anyway. But after he got off the phone, the man thought about his wife, and how they quit drinking together twenty years ago, saved a wrecked marriage and a couple of lives gone bad, and they used to do a lot of work together helping other drunks get sober. But the wife got sick and he spent more and more time taking care of her, and less and less time going to meetings and working with other drunks. And then she died and he was all alone. So he'd decided to cash in his chips, but then he got this phone call. He said he had forgot how good it felt to help somebody. After the call he poured the whiskey down the sink and called his sponsor. He hadn't talked to him in years, but he called him, and then he went to his sponsor's house and spent the night on the couch, and the next morning they went to a meeting. And then he said the strangest thing of all. He said that that night—sleeping on his sponsor's couch—he dreamed that he was walking along the cliffs at Lake Tahoe, and he was looking down into the water. And the bottom of the lake, he said, was golden sand. And when he looked down, he saw the shadow of an angel. And though he looked all around, he could not see the angel anywhere, just the shadow, there in the sand, on the bottom of the lake.

Well you can imagine the fright that gave me. And I tell you something—I've thought about that night, and that meeting, and those dreams, every day since.

And now we meet, you and I, and we sit down for coffee, and your hands are shaking, and you've got child support to pay, and bills to pay, and the devil to pay, and what-the-hell-all else is gone wrong in your life. And your skin is yellow and your eyes are red, and the veins light up on your face like a roadmap, and your lips are papery, and your sweat stinks like cheap whiskey, and you've got pains up here where your liver's got hard. Or maybe not. Maybe you're just a regular Joe and we met at work, or in the aisles of the grocery store, or walking our dogs in the park. But either way, I look pretty normal to you. And when we talk, I talk about normal things like my house, my job, my wife. Then I tell you this story about getting out of jail, and dreams of angels we can't see, and some guy thinking about blowing his brains out, and it all seems pretty weird. It's hard to believe.

But let me tell you what else you can't see. You can't see me when I was little, in the bathroom with my mother, sticking my fingers down her throat to make her puke because she OD'd on pills again. And you can't see me with welts on my back from the beatings she gave me with a stud belt, or hiding in the neighbor's yard in the rain because she'd gone off and locked me out of the house, again, and I was too ashamed to ask for help. And you can't see me stealing booze from her liquor cabinet and watering down the bottles so she wouldn't know. And you can't see inside my head to know that when I drank, I felt different, and different was better than what I felt the rest of the time. And you can't see that when I took that first drink, I was like a truck without brakes. And you can't see me failing out of high school and joining the navy, or sitting in the brig in San Diego because I went AWOL on a blackout in Tijuana, or me walking around in little circles to keep from nodding out OD'd on heroin, or face down in an alley somewhere. And you can't see me beating my wife, or getting run off jobs for stealing or drinking or general incompetence. You can't see me packing my things and slinking away in the middle of the night, the foreclosure notice nailed on my door, or lying to my son about why I couldn't visit him on weekends, or fighting with the cops, riding in a paddy wagon, hot blood running down my face, eyes swelled shut, cuffs cutting off the circulation to my hands, singing "Born on the Bayou" at the top of my lungs all the way downtown. You can't see me carrying a pistol and robbing some poor bastard who stopped at the wrong ATM, or staring at the water stains on the ceiling of that little cell in Petaluma. You can't see me this way at all.

The world is full of things we can't see. Some of them we could track down and read in newspaper accounts and court records. Others we could ask around and hear from first-hand from eye-witnesses. And then there are things like angels, things we accept on faith, if we believe in them at all. And I can tell you for sure I know the meaning of my dream, although I did not know it then. I had no way of knowing that I—fresh out of jail, without even a change of clothes to my name—could be of any use to anyone. But I was. I saved somebody's life, even if I didn't mean to. And that fact alone has sustained me all these years. There are many things we cannot see, but the hardest thing is to see ourselves as we really are—good or bad. And if you have trouble seeing me in Petaluma, California, writing under a streetlight in the parking lot of Saint Francis' Church at five o'clock in the morning, then imagine my surprise when I realized that the angel in that dream was me. That is why I could only see the shadow. And there it is. There is that, and everything else you don't know about me.

Tiger Hunting

Mr. Jindal arrived at Bandhavgarh exhausted by the trip from Mumbai. The train ride to Kitni was almost sixteen hours, and that was followed by a brutal jeep ride of almost four hours covering the 120 kilometers up into the hills to the village and the resort and the tiger reserve. The road was in impossibly poor repair, almost beyond imagination, even for an Indian highway; a single semi-paved lane rutted and potholed to the limit of one's endurance. The air was filled with choking clouds of red dust and the noxious fumes of India's notoriously poor-grade diesel fuel, and traffic was heavy, with the jeep constantly slowing to pass lumbering Tata trucks, or people on bicycles, or walking, or driving teams of oxen, or herding cattle, or just plain lunatics, the sadhus, who professed to be wandering holy men but were worse than anything when it came to getting out of the way. And there had been another passenger in the jeep, an American, Mr. Weiss, a taciturn man who had said nothing the entire way from Kitni, alternately dozing and looking intently at the countryside, and he had brought a large backpack and a suitcase, so the jeep was crowded with baggage, and Mr. Jindal had to ride in the back seat, and it was hot and cramped and suffocating, and he was thoroughly exhausted by the time he arrived in Banhavgarh, and his neck hurt.

When Mr. Jindal arrived at the resort, porters took his bags to one room and Mr. Weiss' bags to another, and Mr. Jindal liked his room, with its cheery view of the hills, and brightly polished wooden floors, and elegant walls of stone veneer and fresh white plaster, hung with gay pictures of Maharajas on horseback hunting tigers with spears, or courtly scenes of handsome Rajas seducing buxom Indian maids under the bemused eyes of doting servants. And the furniture was upholstered in expensive, brightly-colored cotton prints, all clean, all new. Even the bathroom was freshly-tiled with gleaming modern fixtures. Above the dresser hung an ornately carved gold-gilded mirror, and Mr. Jindal paused and looked at himself. His face was thin and evenly proportioned, his nose straight, his eyes dark, wide and intelligent, his mahogany skin without a wrinkle. His hair had gone white, the price he'd paid for long hours of hard work and the worries commensurate with his career as a businessman. And now, he thought, at the end of it all, he had time and the money to enjoy life, and he was grateful that he still had his health.

But evidently there was a mix-up and the owner came around and ordered Jindal's and Weiss' rooms reversed. The second room was more modest, with concrete floors overlaid with peeling linoleum imitation-wood parquet, and plastered walls sorely in need of paint, worn furnishings that didn't match, a double bed that sagged badly in the middle, and a bathroom with a showerhead that dripped cold water constantly. And the room faced the road, where passing traffic raised clouds of dust that drifted through the open windows. When the arrangements were finally straightened out, Mr. Jindal surveyed the room, and despite the disparity between the two, felt the relief of a traveler at the end of a long day's journey. He inquired of the porter about dinner (it was not to be served until 8:00 PM, but there would be tea at 6:00) and checked his watch (4:00 PM). He tipped the porter twenty rupees, took a cool shower, and lay down to take a nap.

No sooner had Mr. Jindal dozed off than the door burst open, and the porter reappeared bearing four heavy suitcases and clutching a large camera bag in his teeth. From the front porch Mr. Jindal heard a man abusing the porter, "Careful, that camera costs more than you'll earn in *two* lifetimes."

The porter stumbled into the room, dropped the suitcases with evident relief, and set the camera bag gingerly on the edge of the bed. Behind him, in the doorway, Mr. Lalwani appeared. Mr. Lalwani was short and fat, bald as a cricket bat on top, but with long, black hair (obviously dyed) sprouting thick from the sides of his head and combed back over his ears. He wore a grey and red plaid knit vest over a white shirt with a blue tie, grey slacks, and black shoes polished to an obsidian gleam. He wore thick, horn-rimmed glasses, too, and Mr. Jindal was immediately reminded of old photos of Chairman Mao.

Mr. Lalwani's eyes darted about the room. In a moment, they lighted upon Mr. Jindal, now sitting up in bed. Placing his hands on his hips he demanded, "Who are you?"

"I'm Mr. Jindal."

"And what are you doing in my room?"

"This is my room, sir." Mr. Jindal bit his lip. The deferential sir had been an inadvertent slip. He added hastily, "there must have been some kind of mix-up."

"We'll see about that," Lalwani said, and he turned on his heels and walked out of the room, calling from outside for the porter. The porter, who had stood to one side during the exchange, smiled weakly at Mr. Jindal, then picked up the camera bag and gripped it in his teeth and carefully stacked the suitcases so he could cradle one under each arm while holding one in each hand. He grunted and staggered as he lifted them. He left the room without closing the door.

Mr. Jindal sighed and checked the clock by the bed. It was only 4:45, but he decided to dress for tea anyway. Perhaps, he thought, he could take a short walk into the village; it might help him relax. He

75

dressed in his best white traditional *salwar-kurta* and began to fasten his sandals.

But before he could finish, the porter returned and set the suitcases on the floor and the camera bag on the bed. Mr. Lalwani followed. "There has been a mistake," Lalwani said, facing the porter and not Mr. Jindal. "The management has overbooked and I must share *my* room. I am very angry. I expected better service than this. If there was another hotel . . . but there are no better choices in this wilderness. Unless," and he cocked his eyebrow and looked at Mr. Jindal from the corner of his eye, "you decide to take a room in the village. It's probably less expensive, anyway."

Mr. Jindal finished fastening his sandals and stood up. "It is a large room," he said, "and I am all right with sharing. I'm sure the management will compensate us for any inconvenience they have caused." He extended his hand to Mr. Lalwani. "I am Mr. Jindal."

Mr. Lalwani grunted a guttural, "Enh," then removed his shaving kit from a suitcase and went into the bathroom and closed the door. Mr. Jindal hesitated. The porter was still standing beside the open front door. He, also, looked confused. Mr. Jindal took out his wallet and handed the porter two ten-rupee notes. The porter bowed slightly and closed the door. The bathroom door opened. "Lalwani," Mr. Lalwani said, but he said it with a curious, Chinese accent, so that it sounded like *La Wa Nee*. Then he closed the door, and a moment later Mr. Jindal heard Mr. Lalwani drawing a bath.

It was a pleasant walk of about a kilometer into town. The road wound down into a dry ravine and then out again, past a few scattered houses, and Mr. Jindal saw no one but a few women in colorful saris harvesting wheat in a distant field. He was surprised to find Mr. Weiss sitting at a table outside the village coffee shop. The village itself wasn't much, a cluster of low huts built of mud bricks with clay tile roofs. The walls of the better homes were plastered with dried cow dung, the rest smeared with ordinary mud. Folklore held that dried dung discouraged mosquitoes, thereby reducing the risk of malaria, but Mr. Jindal doubted this. The coffee shop was built just like the houses except that it had a dusty, rusting roof of corrugated tin. There were three plastic tables set outside along with a dozen plastic chairs.

Mr. Weiss was short and silver-blonde, slightly overweight, but not grossly obese like many of the foreign visitors Mr. Jindal had met. Weiss had a leathery, worn complexion accentuated by the red road dust from the afternoon's ride, now blackening with sweat from the afternoon heat. He was dressed carelessly in denim shorts and a khaki shirt with tattered hiking boots and a battered green canvas hat. He motioned for Mr. Jindal to sit down. "Chai?" he asked, "it's quite good."

Mr. Jindal nodded appreciatively and sat down. "Namaste," he said, bowing slightly because they had not been formally introduced, even though they had ridden together.

"Tif Weiss," Weiss said, extending his hand.

"Sharad Jindal." He shook Weiss' hand and noted that, like many Americans, Weiss affected a belligerent, crushing grip. "I suppose you've come to see the tigers?"

"Yes," Weiss looked away. The proprietor of the café came out, and Weiss held up two fingers. The proprietor nodded and went back inside.

Mr. Jindal cleared his throat. "First trip to India?" he asked.

"Yes," Weiss replied.

"You are from America."

"Yes."

"What state?"

"Vermont, but I've traveled all over."

Mr. Jindal nodded. "I was photographing in Alaska last fall, near Juneau. It was beautiful. I got some very nice pictures of bear and eagle feeding on the salmon."

"I've never been to Alaska."

"You must go sometime. I've photographed tigers and lions and leopards, both in India and in Africa, Tanzania, Kenya, Namibia. I even photographed a snow leopard in Tibet, very rare. But nothing I have seen was half as intimidating as the brown bear."

"I saw one once, in Montana, from a distance. I was on horseback and the bear was on the other side of a narrow canyon. It looked as big as my horse, and I was glad it wasn't any closer."

"The one animal I would like to photograph most," Mr. Jindal said, "is the black panther."

Weiss cocked his head. "Why's that?"

"Not only are they rare, but from a photographer's perspective, they're nearly impossible to capture on film. You see, they lodge in trees, up in the shadows. And half the trick of photography is getting the light right. It's a delicate art. You must plan your shot carefully, but being in the right place at the right time is just part of the game. You must have the right equipment and compose and time your shot. And the subject must cooperate. I've gone to the Everglades three times to photograph panthers, and only once seen one, and that was just a fleeting glimpse in the shadows. I'm going again in January."

Weiss said, "I'm no photographer. I just came because I heard I could see tigers in the wild."

"What do you do?"

"I'm in I.T."

"N.I.T?"

"I.T. Internet technology. I teach business professionals to use their computers efficiently. The average user uses only 5% of his or her computer's potential. I teach them to use more, even if it's only shortcuts. It makes them more productive."

"I see. I'm not very good with computers myself. My son practically lives on his, but I still count on my fingers." Mr. Jindal laughed.

"And what do *you* do?" Weiss asked.

"I own a photography store in Mumbai."

"A studio?"

"No, photography is my hobby. In my store I sell cameras and darkroom equipment, printers, papers, chemicals, supplies. If you use it in photography, I sell it." Mr. Jindal took a card from his wallet and passed it to Mr. Weiss.

Weiss put the card in his shirt pocket without reading it.

The waiter brought more chai and Mr. Jindal sipped, then nodded his approval. "It's good," he said.

Weiss said, "Until I came to India, I'd never had chai. Now I like it almost as much as coffee."

They finished their drinks and Mr. Jindal stood up. "Perhaps I'll see you at dinner?"

"I'll look for you," Weiss said.

* * * * *

The 'resort' consisted of a dozen bungalows clustered around a central lodge, a darkly lit but attractive room, wood-paneled, with immaculate white linens and polished silver table settings. The most outstanding feature of the room was that there was a tree growing through the middle of it, the structure of the lodge tying into the tree as a living, central pillar. The walls were decorated with wildlife pictures, primarily tigers. Mr. Jindal guessed that they were taken by guests at the reserve. Most of the pictures were amateurish; either the light was wrong, or the tigers were obscured in peculiar ways by grass or underbrush, or the composition was out of balance. He could tell from the clarity of the focus that most of the photographers used expensive equipment and had some degree of competence, but there was only so much you could learn in a class. Photography, he felt, required something more than a working knowledge of shutter speeds, ASAs, focal lengths, and aperture settings. There was that intangible element called *the photographer's eye*, and that was something you either had or you didn't have, but it couldn't be taught. Perhaps this was the thing, he reflected, that kept him coming back to photograph wildlife again and again. It wasn't that he was going to take a photo that had never been taken. Even the black panther had been done, albeit rarely. Once in a great while someone would photograph an animal that was believed extinct or engaged in a behavior that had not been previously documented. On the wall of the lodge, for instance, were two photographs of tigers in trees, a mother and her cub. So far as Mr. Jindal knew, tigers didn't climb trees. But there it was, in living color, proof that they did, unless this was one of those Photoshop manipulations, digital forgeries, like his son liked to manufacture in his spare time. Mr. Jindal shook his head. Computer wizards might someday transubstantiate these shams by the thousands, near-perfect simulations of creatures in places they could never be doing things they could never do—like Vishnu appearing as human body with a boar's head, or the Monkey God, or Ganesh the elephant-headed God, or an eight-armed Kali with her scimitar and necklace of severed heads. But no matter how clever they were with machines, there was one thing they could never offer: that serendipitous moment when equipment, nature, and artist came together in a perfect holy trinity. What was it, Mr. Jindal wondered, that made the photographer stay his trigger-finger a split-second, just long enough for the tiger look up and bare her teeth or narrow his eyes, or pause in the only patch of light in otherwise shrouded brush, or the instinct that said, later on in the darkroom, crop here, so that the picture was theoretically out-of-balance but in way that was aesthetically stunning? Perhaps it was the quest to understand this phenomenon that kept him coming back to the wild.

The door opened and Mr. Jindal looked up, expecting Mr. Weiss. But instead he saw Mr. Lalwani standing in the entry, looking around the various tables, appearing slightly bewildered. Most of the other guests were Europeans or Australians—Anglos, all of them. Mr.

Lalwani's face soured but brightened when it lit upon Mr. Jindal. He hurried to the table and sat down on the opposite side.

"Good evening," Mr. Jindal said.

Mr. Lalwani grunted, a distinctive Chinese mannerism, then replied, "Good evening," with an affected Chinese accent.

A waiter appeared with soup and glasses of chilled water. Mr. Lalwani sniffed at the soup, then shooed away the water. "Bring me a bottle," he said. "Unopened." He took a tentative spoonful of soup, then finished the bowl, slurping loudly as he ate.

Weiss came in, saw Mr. Jindal and Mr. Lalwani, and walked across the room to their table. "Mind if I join you?" he asked. Without waiting for a reply, he sat down.

Mr. Jindal nodded.

Mr. Lalwani grunted and said, in Hindi, "Goddam White ought to sit at his own table."

"Thank you," Weiss said. "*Shukryia.*"

Lalwani looked away and, scowling, muttered something Mr. Jindal could not make out.

"So tell me," Mr. Jindal asked, "what part of India are you from?"

A line of waiters came in from the kitchen, each carrying a polished steel bowl. The sweet and spicy aroma of Indian cooking filled the room like incense. The waiters allowed Mr. Lalwani to serve himself first—potato curry, dal, rice, mutton in gravy, vegetable paneers, and roti. There was plenty of food for all of them. However, Mr. Lalwani loaded his plate with more than any two guests could have eaten, and Jindal and Weiss ate, out of modesty, less.

When he had finished heaping his plate, Mr. Lalwani replied, "My family came from Gorakhpur, in the north, but I have lived in Hong Kong for nearly fifty years."

"And what do you do in Hong Kong?" Weiss asked.

"Me? Ahh, nothing. I go to board meetings now and then. I own a few manufacturing companies, but mostly I travel around taking pictures."

"What kind of manufacturing?"

Mr. Lalwani paused, his fork suspended in mid-air. "Manufacturing," he said, and then he continued eating.

Weiss nodded, but didn't speak again until dinner was finished. Afterwards, he stood up, nodded to Mr. Jindal, and said, "Good night, gentlemen."

Once Weiss was gone Mr. Lalwani became conversational, almost animated. For nearly a half-hour he regaled Mr. Jindal with his photographic escapades, including the details of three previous trips to Bandhavgarh, all of which resulted in tiger sightings. "In fact," Mr. Lalwani confided, "I'm making a presentation of my photography to the Royal Society of Hong Kong as soon as I leave Bandhavgarh. It is a special honor to be invited to join the Royal Society, you know, especially for a resident of *Indian* origin."

Later on, in their room, Mr. Lalwani booted his laptop and showed Mr. Lindal the power point presentation he had carefully prepared. In addition to tiger, Mr. Lalwani had photos of nearly every imaginable game animal: black bear, brown bear, polar bear, panda bear, elephant, hippo, rhinoceros (both one and two-horned), giraffe, zebra, an assortment of twenty-odd rare deer, elk, moose, caribou, mountain goats, wild boar, an exhaustive collection of all twenty-five sub-species of cobra (both male and female), seven different types of crocodiles, and more than eighty rare songbirds. But without a doubt, the bulk of Mr. Lalwani's collection were cats: Indian and African lions, South American jaguars, African leopards, snow leopards, lynx, manx, ocelots, cheetahs, American mountain lions, and (and Mr. Jindal's heart sank when he saw it), a perfectly executed shot of a black panther crouched on a branch so close it seemed the photographer could have reached out and stroked the cat's gleaming fur. "This," Mr. Lalwani said, tapping the image of the panther on the screen with his finger, "is the grand finale, the coup-de-grace! Do you know how long it took me to get this picture?"

Mr. Jindal shook his head.

"Ha!" Lalwani shouted, slapping himself on the thigh. "Half-a-day! I bribed one of the park rangers to tranquilize him with a dart gun. He had a radio collar on, too, so he was easy to track. I took the collar out with Photoshop. You could look under a microscope and you'd never know it was there."

* * * * *

Mr. Jindal slept well that night, though he was aware Mr. Lalwani was tossing and turning, sometimes snoring loudly beside him. When Mr. Jindal got up to use the bathroom, he found an open medicine bottle containing little blue pills on by the sink. He held one up to the light. There were no markings on it, and the writing on the bottle was in Chinese.

A porter woke them at five and they dressed hurriedly, donning jackets and hats because the hill country was *much* cooler in the morning. Mr. Lalwani insisted on sitting in the front of the jeep. Weiss and Mr. Jindal sat in back, along with Mr. Patankar, the resort's resident tiger expert. At the entry to the park they were joined by a park guide, who rode standing on the back bumper while holding on to the jeep's roll bar. For nearly an hour they crisscrossed the reserve at breakneck speed, pausing only to exchange notes with the drivers of other jeeps from the other resorts in the area. The drivers, guides, and Mr. Patankar conversed animatedly in Hindi, which Weiss did not understand. From time to time Weiss asked what they were saying. "They are tracking the tigers," Mr. Jindal replied.

At other times the driver abruptly stopped and shushed his passengers. They would sit for several minutes, then reverse the jeep a few hundred yards and sit some more, or drive forward a ways and stop, or zip around to the other side of the ridge and wait there. The country air was chilly, and Mr. Jindal needed to use the bathroom. He squirmed in his seat. His right leg had gone numb.

"What the hell are they doing now?" Weiss asked.

"Sambhar deer," Mr. Patankar replied. "They make a distinctive call when the tigers are on the prowl."

"A call?"

"Yes, a little high-pitched 'Oh!' sound. If you listen you can hear it."

After a minute, Weiss admitted that he could, though he wasn't sure if the deer were sounding an alarm about the tigers or the jeeps.

A few hundred meters down the road Mr. Patankar slowed the driver and pointed at the road: tiger tracks, very clear in the thick dust. "The tiger likes trails," Mr. Patankar explained. "He can't tell the difference between a road and a natural trail. He has no fear of men or jeeps. That's one reason he makes easy prey."

"You mean we could drive right up to one?" Weiss asked.

"Happens all the time. We've even had them charge the jeeps, though they seldom bite."

"How seldom is seldom?"

"Show him your arm," Lalwani grunted from the front seat.

Patankar rolled up his right sleeve and showed Weiss three large puncture marks on his forearm. The scars were bright red and thickly granulated.

"A tiger did this?"

Patankar waived his hand dismissively. "It was not such a big thing. We think she had been hit by a car the night before out on the highway. She had gone crazy, digging up dirt and clawing trees. She was bleeding from the mouth, clearly injured. A jeep came along with some tourists, and the tiger charged. The driver and the guide ran away, but the tourists froze. The tiger grabbed one of them, and they had a tug-of-war—the tourists and the tiger. We came round the bend, and I got out and grabbed the tiger by the tail—"

"You grabbed the tiger?"

"What else was I going to do? Feeding tourists to the tigers would be very bad for business and for the tigers."

"Not to mention the tourists."

"Yes, bad for them, too. But when people and tigers interact, tigers always get the worst of it. Anyway, I grabbed the tiger until she let go of the tourist, and then she roughed me up a bit. That was all. She left, and the rangers closed the park until they killed her."

Weiss clapped Mr. Patankar on the shoulder. "Hat's off to you, buddy," he said. "A man who'll grab a tiger by the tail can ride in my jeep anytime."

"Really, it's not such a big thing. Tigers can behead a sambhar with a single slash of their paw, but they rarely attack people. They have more to fear from us than we do from them."

"You mean poachers?"

"Yes. Poachers take almost half the tigers born in the park."

"For the pelts or the thrill?"

"Neither. Most of the time it's villagers killing a tiger that's taken to lifting cattle. The pelts are practically worthless; get caught with one and you lose it and draw a prison sentence. Besides, one tiger equals one pelt. Not much profit there. The professionals are after the bones. Grind them into powder and sell them on the black market. It's big medicine in China, you know. Claim is they're an aphrodisiac."

"An all-natural Viagra?"

"Something like that. But there's no thrill to hunting a tiger. Go hide in the bamboo, the tiger will find you."

"Is that what the poachers do?"

"No, it's worse than that. The tiger kills a deer or a cow. Then it hangs around the carcass feeding off it until it's gone. All the poacher has to do is sight the circling vultures, then poison the carcass. Much quieter than a gun, and just as effective. Safer, in fact."

Weiss nodded.

Another jeep passed, and the drivers exchanged notes. The driver turned around and followed the second jeep around the bend and up a trail hewn from solid rock climbing to the top of a steep escarpment.

"We're in luck," Mr. Patankar said. "They've sighted a family, a female and four cubs. They'll put on quite a show."

Within a few minutes, nearly a dozen jeeps converged on the hilltop. Then three elephants appeared, lumbering down the road in a row. The *mahuts* paused, in turn, to consult with Patankar. Then the *mahut* riding the largest elephant goaded it off the road and, in just a few seconds, even the sound of it crashing through the brush was lost. A few minutes later the elephant returned, and all of the *mahuts* guided their elephants alongside various jeeps. The passengers scrambled up from their seats to the rollbars, and from the rollbars onto the platforms saddling the elephants. The park guides and the drivers steadied the more infirm passengers, Mr. Lalwani for one, and then passed them their cameras when they were safely aboard.

Weiss' eyes bugged when he saw Mr. Lalwani's camera—the lens looked like something you might launch rockets from. Then he saw that Mr. Jindal had the exact same camera and lens, as did most of the other tourists. Weiss whistled softly to himself and looked at his puny Olympus digital.

Mr. Jindal handed his camera to Mr. Weiss and climbed onto the platform. Weiss' arm bucked under the weight. "How the hell do you hold this thing?" he asked.

Jindal smiled. "It takes some getting used to, but when you feel the adrenaline, you forget the weight of the camera. In fact, there's something to be said for holding a substantial lens—it is less affected by vibration. It actually makes your hand steadier."

And by the time I'm able to afford a $25,000 ensemble, Weiss thought, *my hands will need all the stability they can get.*

Weiss passed the camera to Patankar who handed the camera up to Jindal. Weiss stood up on the seat to climb on, but Lalwani spoke sharply to the *mahut,* who kicked the elephant in the back of the head and got it moving. Weiss nearly tumbled off the jeep. Patankar and the guide caught hold and steadied him. As the elephant lumbered into the brush, Jindal looked back and shrugged his shoulders.

Once they were out of earshot, Jindal asked Lalwani why he hadn't allowed Weiss onto the platform.

"Too crowded. He'll mess up my shots. He's not taking pictures, anyway. Let him wait."

Weiss regained his balance, sat down, and said nothing.

"They'll come back for you," Patankar said.

Weiss didn't answer.

"Sometimes the *mahuts* do that, you know, only take two at a time." The lie was transparent. Weiss had only to look at the other tourists climbing three, even four at a time onto the platforms to know otherwise, but he maintained a stoic silence. He took out a pair of field glasses and began studying the surrounding foliage.

Patankar watched Weiss, and guessing he was looking for songbirds said, "*tot rungi*, jungle wrens."

Weiss said nothing.

Patankar climbed out of the front seat and into the back. He patted Weiss on the shoulder. "Let me tell you a story," he said. "Two years ago Lalwani came out here for the first time. I had heard rumors about him. Guide talk, you know, 'drinking their whiskey' things. I had actually seen his work in exhibitions; he's a world-class photographer. Our second day out he was paired up with me, a couple of French girls, and an old Norwegian gentleman named Halvor. The girls might not have been twenty, and Halvor was seventy if he was a day. We rode around all morning without much luck—the tigers just didn't want to be seen. It was most unusual, really. The big male, V2, kept roving back and forth along the ridge. After a while, Halvor had to get out to pee. The guide wasn't very happy about having the guests tramp about in a wood full of tigers. It's not a good idea. But that day the guide was especially uneasy about things, and he insisted that Halvor stay close to the jeep. Well, the girls and I looked the other way, out of modesty, I suppose. And I was looking away. But then Lalwani grabs his camera and starts taking pictures. *The bastard,* I thought. I was about to say something, but when I looked, I saw that there was a leopard crouched on a branch not three feet above the spot where Halvor was relieving himself. I was stunned. And while Lalwani clicked away, the leopard reached down and tried to swat the hat off Halvor's head. By this time, all of us were looking, but none of us said a word. Tongue-tied, the lot of us. I can't speak for the others, but I was afraid to startle the thing. Halvor zipped up his pants, completely oblivious, got into the jeep, and the driver started it up, and we shot out of there. Nobody ever told him, either, not that I heard about.

"That night, after dinner, I asked Lalwani why he didn't say anything. The man could have been killed. 'And miss a shot like that?' he replied. Ask him about it, he'll show you."

"Right," Weiss said.

Jindal and Lalwani were gone nearly a half-hour. When they returned, Mr. Lalwani climbed down, grinning and grunting. Patankar asked if he'd seen tigers and Lalwani replied that he had "got some good shots." Jindal handed Lalwani's camera down to Patankar, then motioned for Weiss to join him, and they rode back into the bamboo.

If it were possible to say seeing tigers in the wild was disappointing, Weiss would have said that. Anticlimactic. The tiger stretched in feline repose, soaking up the morning sun on a bare rock. The *mahut* goaded the elephant right to the tiger. The tiger was larger than Weiss had imagined—a two-year-old cub was nearly full grown—and it paid them virtually no notice. The elephants circled the tiger while the tourists clicked away with their cameras. Except that there were no walls, the scene could have taken place at any decent zoo. Occasionally the tiger looked around and once licked her paw. And there was a moment—though it only lasted a second—when the tiger had looked up, annoyed, and made eye contact with Weiss. But that moment was something Weiss would never forget. It was a look that said, "I could rip your head off if I wanted." After ten minutes the *mahut* turned to Weiss, and hesitated.

"If you want to stay longer," Jindal whispered, "you have to pay more."

Weiss looked at the tiger, eyes closed, dozing, not paying them the slightest attention; the circling elephants, tearing off the tender clumps of young bamboo and eating as they thrashed around in the brush; the tourists, outfitted in the finest REI jungle-adventure clothing money could buy, their motor-driven super-cameras whirring and clicking. "Let's go," he said.

On the way back to the lodge, Lalwani spoke animatedly in Hindi to Jindal. The talk was about photography, particularly equipment, and despite the fact that he sold cameras for a living, Mr. Jindal deferred, at least outwardly, to Lalwani's opinions.

* * * * *

And that was the way the first day passed, and the second, and the third, only that Mr. Jindal saw less and less of Weiss. Weiss began to ride in jeeps with the European tourists and even missed one of the jungle excursions altogether. When Jindal inquired, the head porter said Weiss had gone on a hike to a temple complex at the top of Bandhavgarh Hill. Weiss took his meals late, and alone, and seldom spoke to anyone.

But on the morning of the fourth day Jindal sought out Weiss in his room, early, before the morning ride. "I hope that I'm not disturbing you," he said.

Weiss stood by the door, bleary-eyed, half-dressed, wearing only shorts and socks. The porters had already been around bringing the guests coffee. Mr. Jindal could see that the room, so cheerful and bright a few days ago, had taken on some of Weiss' taciturn demeanor. A computer screen on the dresser by the bed bathed the room in watery blue light, and there were clothes and notebooks and things strewn haphazardly about. It occurred to Mr. Jindal that Weiss might have been up all night.

"What do you want?" Weiss asked.

"May I come in?"

Weiss opened the door wide enough to allow Jindal to enter. "Would you like some coffee?" Weiss asked.

"No thank you," he said, "actually, I can't stand the coffee here."

Weiss laughed, an honest, child-like laugh, and Jindal realized it was the first time he had seen Weiss' brighter side. Until then, he wasn't sure Weiss had one.

"Imagine," Weiss said, "a five-star resort serving Sanka decaf. Here, I brought my own," and he poured Jindal a cup from a small carafe.

Jindal tasted the coffee—it was milky and sweet, true Indian style, just like he liked it. He raised the cup slightly in Weiss' direction. "This tastes like French Market coffee," he said.

"It is," Weiss replied. "You've been to New Orleans?"

"Yes. I went to an exhibition there in 1999."

"Photography?"

"Equipment."

"And you liked it?"

"I loved it, but then, I always liked America. I have a brother there, you know."

"I didn't know."

"In Sarasota, Florida."

"And what does *he* do?"

"He was a doctor, but he's retired now. I'm going to visit him soon, he's advancing in years."

Weiss refreshed their cups, then sat down on the edge of the bed and scratched his face sleepily. "You're not close?"

"How did you guess?"

"Just a feeling."

Jindal opened his mouth, then shut it again.

87

"You can tell me, if you want," Weiss said.

Jindal smiled. "We quarreled when we were young. He wanted to go to America and make his fortune. I wanted to go to college myself, but one of us had to stay here and take care of our parents. It was his responsibility—he was the older brother—but he was insistent about it. He was always stubborn, but my father said there was time enough to send us both to college, and so my brother went to Berkeley and earned his Bachelor's, then to UCLA to medical college, and he married an American girl, and they had children, and he never came home. And my father fell ill, and the responsibility for his care—and even my brother's education—fell to me. I took over my father's shop, just like my son is taking over after me." Jindal folded his hands on his lap and looked about the room. He could see on the computer that Weiss had been writing.

Weiss got up and poured himself another cup of coffee.

"But that was a long time ago," Jindal said. "How do you say it, *water over the dam*?"

"Something like that," Weiss said.

"Actually, I came to talk about Mr. Lalwani."

"What about him?"

"He has a small problem."

"With all his problems, a small one would hardly stand out."

Mr. Jindal smiled, then set his cup on the counter. "It's his computer, actually. He has a presentation to make in Hong Kong tomorrow evening, a very important presentation, and now his laptop is causing him problems. There is no place here for him to fix it and no way to get it to someone who can. I remembered you said that you worked on computers, and I was wondering if I could prevail upon you to fix it, as a favor to me."

"So why doesn't he ask me himself?"

"Would you help him if he asked you?"

"I'd tell him to go fuck himself."

"I suspect he knows that. In any event, he's too proud to ask, even if he knew you would say yes."

"So screw him."

"But he didn't ask me, Mr. Weiss. I came on my own."

"And what makes you think I won't tell you to piss off?"

"Because I think you are a better person than that."

Weiss got up and rummaged around in a pile of dirty clothes until he found a grey tee shirt. He sniffed under the arms, then put it on. He clapped the floppy green hat on his head. "You don't know me very well."

"I know you well enough."

Weiss offered Jindal another cup of coffee, which Jindal declined by placing his hand over his cup.

"Tell me something," Weiss said. "How can you stand to hang around with that asshole? I can't think of two people more unlike."

"Who can say?" Jindal replied. "There are two kinds of people in the world: walls and mirrors. The walls are easy, they're obstacles to overcome. We get around them, climb over them, knock them down if we have to. They test our will. Sometimes they give us opportunity to grow, especially in tolerance. That's a big thing in India, you know. With fifteen religions and twenty languages, acceptance might be our most important asset."

"Okay."

"The wall is but an annoyance, no worse than a stone in our shoe, but mirrors are another thing altogether. You see, there is nothing more frightening than seeing ourselves for what we are. It's easy to test our resolve when it comes to others. But when the test is about ourselves . . . Lalwani may be difficult to deal with, but aren't the difficult accomplishments the most rewarding?"

"What's to accomplish?" Weiss said. "Tonight I go back to Mumbai, and five minutes after I've gone, I won't remember his name."

"It seems to me he has gotten quite under your skin."

"He doesn't take up as much space in my head as you think."

"So you don't mind helping him with his computer?"

"I didn't say that."

"Either you do or you don't. It's a *yes* or *no* question."

Weiss got up and shut his computer down, then opened the curtains full wide and looked around outside, his back to Jindal.

"Mr. Weiss, after my brother finished college, he never came back to India. He had good excuses. His wife was frail, she worried about the health of *their* children, he had bills to pay, and to provide for *their* future and *their* education. Good reasons, all. India tests your endurance daily: the poverty, pollution, dirt, disease, the sheer weight of the crowds. My father died of cancer, a slow death, and painful, and none of us were happy, and there was much unspoken. My bother got what he wanted, and I didn't. A Muslim friend once told me, 'Allah gives and forgives. Man gets and forgets.' This is both sad and true. My father never asked my brother to come home. I've thought a lot about that, and I learned one very important lesson. Resentment, Mr. Weiss, is like cancer. It kills us, and the other fellow doesn't feel a thing. Tell me, have you seen *The African Queen*?"

"The movie?"

"Yes, with Humphrey Bogart and Katherine Hepburn."

"Sure, I've seen it."

"Do you remember that scene, the one where Bogart wakes up hungover and finds Hepburn pouring out his whiskey?"

"I guess so."

"Do you remember what Bogart says?"

"No."

"He says, 'Miss, don't do that. A man's got to have a little drink every now and then. It's human nature.' And she replies, 'Human nature, Mr. Alnutt, is what we are put on this earth to rise above."

"Okay," Weiss said.

"Do you know who Saint Francis is?"

"The patron saint of AA?"

"I beg your pardon?"

"Just kidding. I know who he is."

"He wrote a famous prayer."

"Yes, about serenity."

"Serenity, yes, but more about acceptance. Did you know he was buried in India?"

"I didn't know that."

"Yes, in Goa. At any rate, think about it. Perhaps our test is to put up with others, as others have put up with us. Or beyond that, to repay others with kindness in excess of what they have shown us. I have begun to understand, in my advancing years, that life is precious and short. I realize, Mr. Weiss, that my brother would have been very unhappy had he stayed in India. And I think that I resented him all those years because he got to leave, and I didn't, even though I have done well, perhaps better than he could have done. But now I look at life differently. It's not about what other people do or even what they do to me. It's about what I do, and what effect I have on the world for being here. And that's the mirror, Mr. Weiss. When the world shows me what I am, and I have to choose what I will do. Think about it. I wouldn't expect Mr. Lalwani to express the slightest bit of gratitude. But it does provide you with the chance to be a better man."

* * * * *

Weiss did not show up at the gate for the morning ride, and Jindal and Lalwani rode alone. Lalwani was aggravated before they left, and when the tigers did not cooperate, his mood soured even more. They cut short the morning excursion. On the way back to the lodge, Lalwani said, "I bought a Mac, four thousand U.S. dollars in Hong Kong. World's best computer, and now this. What will I do? My presentation is tomorrow morning? I will be ruined." But when they returned they found Weiss loitering by the front gate. He gave Jindal a sideways glance, then said to Lalwani, "I hear you have a problem with your computer."

Lalwani nodded, expressionless. Mr. Jindal beamed.

Lalwani led Weiss to his room. There was a Zero-Haliburton briefcase on the bed and Weiss, without waiting for Lalwani, tried to open it. The case was locked. Lalwani took the case and dialed in the combination. Weiss opened it. There was nothing inside but a Hong Kong phone book. Lalwani's face broadened in grin, the first time, Weiss noted, that Lalwani showed him a brighter side.

"Maybe thief take briefcase," Lalwani said, shutting the lid. Then he knelt by the bed and removed the bottom drawer from the nightstand. He reached in and withdrew the laptop. "But not take computer." He set it on the coffee table and motioned for Weiss to sit down.

Weiss sat on the floor while Lalwani booted it up. Lalwani tried to bring up the powerpoint presentation file. The computer flashed a grey dialogue box advising that the program would not start because it could not "locate data files."

"File gone," Lalwani said.

Weiss rested his elbows on his knees and his chin in his hands. "Why did you buy a Mac?" he asked.

Lalwani grunted. "Best computer."

"That depends on what you want it for. Graphics, yes, but it's not the easiest thing to work on. And I'm a PC man, myself."

"But you fix, yes?" There was a hint, Weiss thought, of desperation in Lawani's question.

"Maybe."

Lalwani sat down next to Weiss and took the mouse. He opened Photoshop then called up a file labeled tigers. The screen went black, and moment later the computer began to play Journey's "Eye of the Tiger." A series of images flashed onscreen, all tigers, most shots taken sequentially with a high-speed, motor-driven camera. Tigers emerged from the jungle shadows and circled the photographer. Cubs roughhoused with one another and their mother. A huge male fed on a

91

Sambarh carcass. And in one stunning sequence, a pair of tigers copulated. "Very rare picture," Lalwani said.

When that file finished, Lalwani started another, this one of songbirds. They flashed across the screen in magnificent color and focus, their plumage bright, berries and insects in their beaks. And after that came a series about the high, lonely deserts of Kashmir. And then there was one of nudes, black and whites, most of women, but some of men, and some of men and women together. Weiss leaned closer to the screen. Involuntarily he found himself gasping at the images. Some of the pictures were particularly erotic: especially a series of European models partly clad in native Rajastani costumes. Others were simply beautiful—temples in human form. Weiss was stunned; his eyes brimmed with tears. The only thing he could compare Lalwani's work to was Michelangelo's David. He'd heard Lalwani was good, but this was museum-quality art, shot after shot.

Lalwani nudged Weiss with his elbow. "What you think, eh?"

When the display ended, Weiss asked, "What do you need me for? You can show these and you'll be fine."

Lalwani shook his head. "Presentation my life work, best pictures. This for Royal Academy Hong Kong. Induct as member. I spend many hours make perfect. Cut, touch, fix light, color. And order important, much thought about this picture, that picture. Take time. All put to music. Whole thing like symphony, rise and fall to coup-de-grace."

"Coup-de-grace?"

"Yes. Black panther. Last shot, best shot."

"And you didn't make a back-up?"

Lalwani looked away. "No expect problem. Not finish until few days. Think maybe dust get in hard drive. What you think? You fix?"

Weiss looked at his watch. "I might be able to recover it, but it's going to take time. And I leave this evening. I catch a train to Mumbai."

"I fly Hong Kong tonight. Presentation in morning."

"I'll try," Weiss said, "but you have to leave me alone. I can't work with you watching me."

* * * * *

Mr. Jindal was pleased to hear that Weiss agreed to fix Lalwani's computer. Lalwani fretted all afternoon. They went for the afternoon ride and he forgot to bring water and snacks. He was hypercritical of the driver and guide; nothing they did suited him. There were too close or too far, the light was wrong, their talking disturbed the animals.

When they returned Weiss wasn't in his room. Lalwani dashed to the front desk, but the manager assured him that Weiss had not checked out. He didn't know where Weiss was. Perhaps he had gone to town.

They went back to their room to wait. Jindal sat on the edge of the bed watching Lalwani muttering oaths and stuffing his suitcases. And when Lalwani was packed and the jeep loaded for the trip, Mr. Jindal gently laid his hand on Lalwani's shoulder and reminded him that Weiss was doing him a favor, and that there must be some good reason Weiss had gone, some part he needed, some kind of advice, perhaps?

"In this shit-hole?" Lalwani asked.

Lalwani had just summoned a driver to take him to the village when Weiss appeared, whistling and walking down the road with the laptop tucked under his arm.

Lalwani snatched the computer from Weiss' hands. "Why you go?" he asked.

"The generator was down," Weiss explained.

Lalwani waived the computer in Weiss' face. "Use battery."

"Batteries, yes, but no coffee. The computer may run on batteries, but I was up all night. I needed a clear head to work."

The driver tapped Lalwani on the shoulder. "Time, sir," he said. "You don't want to be late."

Lalwani hesitated.

Weiss said, "But the batteries are nearly exhausted, and if you run them down you'll lose everything. You'll have to charge them in the morning, when you get to Hong Kong. I wouldn't try to boot it now."

"You fix?"

"I fix."

Lalwani stared hard at Weiss, then tucked the laptop into its case and climbed into the jeep.

"Remember," Weiss said, "Charge it. Boot it for the presentation. The hard drive is iffy and I can't promise you more than one boot. Don't start it until you are onstage and ready to go."

"I'll ride with you," Mr. Jindal said. He smiled, shook hands with Weiss, and got into the jeep. As they pulled out into the road he looked back once and nodded.

* * * * *

93

Mr. Jindal stood on the tarmac watching the sun glint off the wings of Lalwani's plane as it banked and headed north towards Kolkata. When it was gone he reached down and loosened his right sandal and shook his foot until a small red pebble fell out. He picked it up and held it to the light, his lips moving silently. Then he threw it away.

* * * * *

Weiss stood in the middle of his hotel room, his things packed. The room was much like he'd found it when he arrived: pretty, but empty. He felt guilty that the management deferred to him as a foreign tourist and put Jindal with Lalwani. Weiss would have been all right with the older room. He might have preferred it. Of course, things could have been worse. What if Weiss had been asked to room with Lalwani? That would have been unacceptable. How Jindal put up with him was beyond comprehension. He thought about Mr. Jindal. Weiss liked him, in spite of his esoteric philosophical ramblings.

He and Jindal had extended invitations to visit each others' homes; his in Vermont, Jindal's in Mumbai. And Jindal would come to America, Weiss knew, at least as far as Florida. But something told Weiss that Jindal would stop in Sarasota on the way to the Everglades. *And who knows?* Weiss thought. Jindal and his brother have a lot of catching up to do. That panther picture might have to wait for another trip. He found that thought curiously reassuring.

Weiss turned and saw his reflection in the mirror. He was getting older. There were lines etched around his eyes; his hair was thinning. But he was still young at heart and strong. And he didn't like Lalwani. *Jindal's a good man*, Weiss thought, *but he's not right about everything*. And Patankar was wrong about a few things, too. There was a thrill to tiger hunting. *Even if you only poisoned the carcass.* Weiss imagined Lalwani in the morning: the posh auditorium and the crowd of pretentious intellectuals, the blank stares on their faces, the guffaws breaking off into an icy silence. Lalwani, the consummate showman, dressed in his most expensive silk suit, his fingers glittering with jewels. His expression would be puzzled—grim awareness dawning like the crimson flush spreading across his face. But the damage was done. *Just like the tiger,* Weiss thought, *the burn in the blood means the end has come.* It only took Weiss a few minutes to find and redirect the missing file. After that, he only had to doctor one picture. He prowled around Lalwani's computer for a few minutes until he found cookies from a porn site—and it had been a nasty one—then he went to work. Cut and paste, a few minutes with Photoshop, and presto: he had a picture of Lalwani for the ages. He deleted the black panther—the last picture in the show—and replaced it with the forgery. What had Lalwani called it? The *coup-de-grace*. "Royal Society my ass," he said. "Take *that,* motherfucker."

Viraaga

The girl is small, even for her young age, and thin—not quite 40 kilos. Her hair is long and straight, black and shiny. Her sweater is black and fleecy, her short skirt black, her leggings and shoes all black, the leggings in a fine lace flower pattern. She wears a thin black cap with a black lace fringe that covers little more than the crown of her head. She carries a light blue cotton bag with a blue-and-white cloth patch in the design of a teddy bear sewn on the outside. A child's bag. The bag looks out-of-place with the girl and the girl looks out-of-place as she steps from the bus and, not seeing the sign that points the way, asks directions from an old woman selling bottles of water and tea and almond milk from a three-legged table perched precariously by the side of the road. Longquan Si. The Dragon Spring Temple. You would think that in a place that has seen as many deaths as this place has, that people would notice. But perhaps in a country with a billion people, one life more or less is not going to make a difference. The woman points down the road and the girl shoulders the bag. "It is a long way," the woman calls after her. "You will want something to drink." The girl stops, looking down the dusty road, then back at the woman. She takes one bottle of each and leaves a twenty yuan note on the table. The woman digs in a purse for change, but the girl walks away and does not look back.

A couple of kilometers off the highway running from Shantou to Jeiyang stands a monastery where the tourists go to have their pictures taken smiling by the fish pond or offering incense in the Shimmering Hall before a gilded statue of the Buddha. The campus's half-dozen buildings glitter red and gold like ornate gift-boxes, the red tiles of the roofs lie smooth like fish scales. The great corner eaves of dark, heavy wood, the *wu yan*, curl upwards like ship's prows plowing an ocean of clouds. The monastery is partly up a steep hill, and local people have evolved the custom of walking backwards up the hill to the entry. Something about life being a blind pilgrimage.

Across the road from the road leading up to the monastery sits a decrepit little amusement park with some puny rides and garishly-painted concrete statues of dragons and lions and elephants. Hawkers line the road selling skewers of spicy chicken or pork, stuffed toys, little bags of hard candy, and drinks.

It was the food that led me, a homeless starving boy, first to the carnival and then to the monastery. Forty-five years ago I came walking up the road and stole some fish from a hawker's grill and escaped up the hill under a barrage of oaths. I slept the night in a small shed and was awakened at five in the morning by two orange-swathed monks. I feared a beating, but instead they beckoned me to follow and led me to a dining hall and there fed me breakfast.

Had I followed that road on past the gate and climbed the hill all the way to the top I would have seen that in the valley beyond lay another monastery, a quiet and un-touristed abode that is far less showy and far more serious in its demeanor. Here, in the quiet shelter of a forested valley, half-a-hundred monks domicile in dormitories and devote their lives to the attainment of Buddhahood—enlightenment. Beyond this monastery stands another mountain—a round, smooth, boulder-clad peak. The monks have built a path to the top, and they are busy carving the boulders that line the path with a thousand scenes of the Buddha's life. No one disturbs them. The carvings are magnificent, but even as one scene is completed and the artist-monks move up that path to begin afresh on a new boulder, the carvings behind begin a slow decay, sprouting thin beards of gray-green moss that will someday erode their features into crumbling sand. The work is like life—a cycle of birth and death with a long decay in between.

Should one venture to the top of *this* path, they would find that behind this mountain stands yet another mountain, the highest in the area; vast and virtually untouched, with a valley in between the two, and a small, swift river; a steep, tree-lined gorge; and a path leading out into a triangular wilderness that spreads fan-like fifty kilometers to the north, into the heart of China. It is a wilderness broken only once—a single east/west highway and accompanying train line, and this some twenty kilometers away. The local people call this place *Gu Yue*, the Valley of Shade Trees.

Few tourists make it to the top of the first hill, and even fewer hike the path past the carvings to the summit of the second mountain, and fewer still descend to the valley below. Fifty or a hundred a year, perhaps. They turn off the highway, leaving a car or motorbike in the parking lot by the amusement park, and when these vehicles have sat long enough to become noticed, the authorities contact the prelate, and the prelate comes looking for me, and I go looking for them. They, these men and women, come to *Gu Yue* to die. It is the place locals go to kill themselves.

It is not an honor, this looking for lost souls in the wood. The task fell to me many years ago because I am the least of my family, a monk with no talent. The monks who took me in that morning so long ago tried to teach me to practice the Middle Way. Most monks progress in mastery of their daily practice. They meditate. They teach. They serve. Some advance in their studies to graduate degrees in useful disciplines—engineering, language and literatures, the arts, even medicine. These might go on to serve as prelates in other monasteries.

I have accomplished nothing in all this time. I cannot manage even simple mathematics, much less recall the endless tomes of ancient history. The only thing I have done perfectly is to have failed.

It was weakness that led me to run away from home, weakness that led me to steal, and the same weakness that led me to flee the disciplined and orderly life of a monk, and seek, instead, solitary consolation in the dark and silent wood. My penance now is to seek these lost souls, the living, if I find them in time; the dead, if I cannot.

As a boy, I spent days and days in truancy, alone in the wood, following the stream to where it split, and the tributaries to where they split, tracing the thousand trickling waterfalls to the caves and springs from which they flowed. I walked animal trails on the plateaus above and climbed the rocky peaks to stand on their precipices and survey eagle-like the valley below. Sometimes I was gone for weeks until hunger or cold drove me back to the shelter of the monastery. It was a lonely torment. When the abbot asked me what I learned on my sojourns I had no answer. What can one learn alone in the wood? That wherever you go, you take your pain with you?

The girl stops at the top of the mountain and sits on a low boulder catching her breath. She takes the bottle of tea from her bag and drinks slowly, one small swallow at a time, pausing in between to breathe. It is a technique she learned for mastering hunger. Feed the body a little and it will stop complaining. She looks to the left, where the sun bathes the red rooftops of the monastery in golden afternoon sunlight. From far below comes the faint and rhythmic chimp-chimp-chimp of hammer-and-chisel on stone. She looks to her right, where a narrow, snake-like path slithers down the shaded slope of the mountain and into the sea of dark green trees. The winter sun is not quite warm, but the valley looks cold. She shivers. She does not want the tea. The thirst has subsided. But as there is no garbage bin, she places the half-empty bottle back into her bag. To litter is to degrade a place with one's presence. She learned long ago to travel quietly and light. The less one leaves behind, the better.

The abbot never rebuked me for deserting my duties, though my fellow monks teased me and called me *Xiao Milarepa*. Xiao means "little" and Milarepa was a famous monk who practiced seclusion, *viveka*. This was the seclusion of the body—a retreat from society. He renounced the world and went up into the mountains to live. In those days, monks sought this seclusion to be rid of distractions. In the wilderness, they could focus on attaining perfection, enlightenment.

I am not enlightened. If I were, I would have mastered my recitations. I could answer the questions the abbot poses before our periods of meditation. I could endure the silence of the stone halls and the slow, measured pace of our breathing exercises. I would not resent the drudgery of our daily chores or detest the thousand flaws I see in my fellows—or loathe myself for seeing them. I would have long ago left a lamp on the wall in the Great Hallway of Illumination, taken my beggar's bowl, and gone out into the world to pass along what I had learned, serving my fellow humans in their struggle to survive. I would have learned discipline, duty, love. I would have found peace. The ultimate goal of Buddhism is not to withdraw from the world but to cease from the attachment to things, from the causes and conditions of suffering, even from the self. This is *viraaga*.

Lying in my bunk, staring up at the ceiling, I am aware of the cracks in the plaster of the illusion of myself that I create. This is what drove me into the wilderness so many years ago, and what still drives me today. It is not the quest for enlightenment, like Milarepa, but the quest for the cessation from suffering. I am nothing if not selfish, though the abbot likes to say, "If I am *nothing*, can I be selfish?" Add to the list that I hate his riddles.

It is four AM. I can tell this from quality of the dark and the silence in the room—from the deep, slow breathing of my sleeping brothers. I can't sleep, as usual. And then I hear footsteps in the hallway outside. The door creaks on its hinges. Soft steps on the stone floor cross the room. A pale, yellow, buttery light flutters in the room. There is a pause and then the gentlest of taps at the foot of my bed. This can only mean one thing.

I sit up slowly and swing my legs to the side. The abbot stares at me. His face is young, smooth, and serious in the light of his candle. I rise and follow him out of the room and down the hallway to the main entry. He nods to where a man, a woman, and a young boy stand impatiently by the door. "There is another one," he says. "The family has come."

They must be wealthy, for they are dressed like western tourists. The man is stocky and broad-shouldered. A northerner. He scowls impatiently. He wears a light khaki photographer's vest over a white shirt and long green trousers. The woman is slightly taller than her husband. Grave-faced. She wears a red-and-black checkered flannel shirt, a black scarf, black leggings with a gray nylon vest. The boy has on a long-sleeved blue sweatshirt with a hood, but over that he wears, open, an orange-and-black nylon jacket. They wear heavy boots, as though they were expecting snow. They carry nylon backpacks, bear water bottles on their belts. They have flashlights and walking sticks. I slip on my sandals and follow them out the door. At the foot of the mountain they stop and take out phones that double as walkie-talkies. They check these to make certain that there is coverage. When I point out the path they brush past me and are quickly out-of-sight up the trail.

The girl sits in the shelter of a boulder and tries to light fire to a stack of twigs. She has a small, orange, plastic lighter. It looks so easy in movies, but somehow she can't get it right. She can't get anything right. The fire sputters and dies. She throws the lighter away. In the book she read, the boy walked three days into the woods before deciding on a spot. It was not the beauty of the place that whispered to him but its inaccessibility. A place from which one could neither return nor be extracted. To disappear as though he had never been, he said. To leave no stain behind. Swallowed. Digested. In the magazine article, it said people unroll lines of colored thread leading from the path to the place, so that they can find their way out if they change their minds or others can find them if they don't. The girl brought no thread. Her mind will not be changed and she doesn't wish to be found. She opens her bag and a bottle falls in the dark and rolls away. The girl gropes on her hands and knees, feeling until she finds it. From the shape of the bottle she can tell it is the tea. She wipes the cap with the hem of her sweater and then drinks the remainder slowly, one sip at a time. She tucks the now-empty bottle back into her bag and then probes deeper. She chooses a chocolate bar and peels away the foil wrap, eating it slowly, savoring every bite as it melts on her tongue. This is good chocolate, one of those things she denied herself for so long, but tonight is special. Tomorrow it will not matter; not food, not her image in the mirror, not the family who loved her to death, nor the boyfriend who did not—evidently—love her enough. Nothing will matter. She lays on the ground with her bag for a pillow and looks up at a sliver of starlit sky that glitters through the cracked canopy of leaves above. The light from above illuminates nothing. In the novel it was beautiful, sublime, a light that warmed the soul and called it to its destiny. Here she feels only the cold, the damp, the tickle of a stray hair on her forehead, the sensation of insects crawling on her legs.

By the time I reach the top of the mountain, dawn is breaking behind me, though the valley below is swathed in shadow and mist. The family is catching their breath. They glare tight-lipped at me. Their urgency, my calm. They see only a problem to be solved, and they will attack this problem with all energy and technology they can command. The man has something called a GPS and software that can find a cell phone in the dark. I see the only solution I know—a long and patient walk. To listen with my heart and ask of the darkness, Which way? It could take hours or days. By noon the family will be exhausted. Already they drink from their bottles, nibble hi-tech snacks peeled from foil wrappers. The do not offer me refreshment, though I have neither pack nor canteen.

"Tell me about your daughter," I say.

The father glares at me. The mother says, "She is too young."

"How old?"

"Seventeen."

"What is she like?"

"Confused," the father replies. A single word spit into the gray light. He stuffs the bottle into its pouch and takes up his walking stick.

"I mean, What is she like?" I say again. When the father narrows his eyes I say, "Is she active? Is she a homebody? Does she play sports? Does she ride a bicycle? Is she a good student? Does she like to read?"

"And what does that have to do with anything?"

I look out over the woods spread below. A mist flows along the ground beneath the trees. The rounded tops of the cork oaks dotting the central valley float like leaf islands in a sea of milk. The father looks down, too, and perhaps for the first time realizes the enormity of the task. A sprawling wilderness of many square kilometers, one small girl. Even with a GPS—who knows? "There are many places to choose from," I say. "If I knew more about the girl, I might make a better guess. And if we find her, I might have a better idea what to say."

The father scowls. "If we find her," he says, "I'll do the talking."

"Have you found many?" the mother asks. Her voice cracks.

Her face is not old, but no longer young. It is the beginning of the end for her, I think. Time will erode her features just like the moss will eat away the carvings we passed on the path below. "Sometimes," I reply. "Sometimes we find them."

"I mean before . . ." her voice trails off.

"Sometimes we get lucky and find them."

The father squints into a flat, black, thin device. "Luck," he says, "is for superstitious fools. Nobody makes it by being lucky." He taps the device with is right hand. He points north. "That way."

I have always been a slow walker, but steady. The family rushes ahead, but time and again they stop and catch their breath and wait for me to catch up. When we pause, they do not speak to me. They have not told me their names. Not even the name of the girl we seek. Perhaps they are embarrassed. They press on, mindful only of a green dot on a black screen. By noon we kneel by the bank of the little river. It is the first of many divides in the river, and from here the paths grow many, narrow and steep. The woman pumps water into their bottles. I drink from a little stream that trickles down the face of a mossy rock. "Aren't you worried about infection?" she asks.

"I drink this water all the time," I say. "But perhaps I am used to it. You are wise to be careful."

She drops a pill into the water, shakes the bottle and watches the pill dissolve. Even the man is sitting down now. He looks like an executive, a morning jogger. He is proud of his stamina, but his strength is drained. He has probably been twenty-four hours without sleep. He looks at me, and for the first time I see something in his face besides impatience. He searches my face and I wonder what he wonders about me. What I think of him? What I know? What I might not be telling them? Can two men be more different?

I pick up a small, orange lighter from the brush. "Does she smoke?" I ask.

The mother shakes her head.

The boy, who until now has not uttered a single word to me, suddenly says "Jeiyang does not do sports. She likes to read. Mostly silly books. Girl books about boys and princesses and singers and love. But she is smarter than people think. She only doesn't get good grades in school because she does not try." He looks at me, his eyes red and sagging.

The father has been tinkering with the GPS. The signal is weak. "The battery is exhausted," he says. But he is the type of man who plans for everything. He has a spare.

102

"The sound of your voice," I say.

The man freezes, the GPS in his hand.

"Your voice," I say again. "Will she call if she hears you, or will she run away?"

The mother and father speak at the same time. "Call." "Run." They look at each other. The boy says nothing. There is a long pause. The water's sound is so pretty this time of day. The morning mist is burned away like last night's dreams. The sky is not cloudy, but not clear, either. High, thin clouds. A white sheet drawn over the face of the earth. The air is grown close and thick but not so cold as before. There is the beginning of a breeze from the north. It will be colder tonight.

"She has been here," the father says. He says it like he knows, but he looks to me for confirmation.

I shrug. "Probably." There is a small scattering of twigs. A spent lighter. Someone was here.

"But you can't tell."

"That is the stuff of movies," I say. I squat and touch the ground. "A thousand years' accumulation of molding leaves does not take impressions. In the mud by the stream, perhaps. Perhaps fresh scrapings up an embankment. A fragment of cloth on the bark of a tree or a bramble. The only way to know for sure," I say, "are things discarded. Clothes and bottles and wrappers and such. Did she bring string?"

"String?" the mother asks.

The father squints into the GPS.

"They sometimes weave trails into the woods when they leave the path," When they look at me I add, "So they can find their way back."

The father and mother look at each other and shrug. The boy says, "I don't think she would think of that."

"And how did you know she was coming here at all?" I ask.

"The book," they say. The father taps the GPS. The signal is fading. It is not his batteries that expire. It's the ones in the girl's phone. One cannot plan for everything.

It is the first night in her life that she has spent outdoors. A whole lifetime of emotion in the dark. Fear, sorrow, anger, exhaustion, hope, despair—and then the dawn. Laughter. It is exhilarating in a way she can't explain—to wake up in the woods cold and wet but to have survived the night. To have done this thing that is so against the rules. Rules by her father. Rules by her mother. Rules by her teachers, her boyfriend, the party, the school, society, all of it. It is probably illegal to even be here, but in the woods, she thinks, in the wilderness, there are no rules. She could take off her clothes. She could dance to any music she wanted. Eat any food she desired. She takes the bottle of water from her bag and drinks greedily, spilling water down her chin and onto the front of her sweater. She looks at the remaining chocolate. Her stomach is tight with hunger but, so what? She is not 37 kilos for nothing. It is nothing to resist hunger. That she can fight. But now she searches the bag with some anxiety. There was a plastic bag and some dry herbs. It is better, the website said, to soak them in water all day, and then strain out the plant matter and drink the liquid that remains. Where is the bag and the herbs? Frantically she upends the bag: a make-up kit, another chocolate bar, a small flashlight, house keys, her i-phone, the pen drive with her homework assignment that she couldn't find last week, a keychain with a green, one-eyed monster, a one-yuan coin, a book of poetry, William Blake, translated into Chinese with the illustrations, a little hardback book of poetry by Li Li. Frantically she searches the ground around her until she spots it. She practically gasps in relief. When she dropped the bottle last night, the bag must have fallen out, too. It lies partially concealed under the outspread tendrils of a trailing purple nightshade. Good thing she woke up thirsty. But she also drank all her water. She looks around, empties the herbs into the empty bottle, then glides down a side path to the river and fills the bottle there. Right away it takes on a sickly, yellowish hue, but whether it is the woodiness of the water or the herbs infusing their magic, she cannot say. She grimaces, then thinks, No matter. If she had mixed the herb with the water she bought yesterday, she could have drunk it just now, but no, this isn't the place. She goes back to the path and her bag and the pile of belongings. The trail forks here, but both branches lead somewhat north. The west side has more morning light. The sun will be warm. It is a pleasant way to die, she thinks, she who has spent too much time in darkness. She gathers her things slowly, placing them in the bag one item at a time. Funny the things we cling to. Everything is in her bag except for the i-phone. Even here there is coverage. Eleven missed calls. Facebook. Twitter. It's all bullshit. What does she care anymore? She looks at the keychain—a gift from a boy—and the phone—a gift from her grandfather. So many things you can do with a phone, he said. Such wonderful tools. It even has GPS.

What I have not told the family is that I have never found a lost soul alive, not one, not on purpose. I give the families hope, but the only ones I have found have been chance wanderers when I wasn't actually looking for anyone. For the rest, my arrival was too late. I have found them hanging in trees or laying on the ground beneath the noose if they had hung long enough for the flesh and bone to yield to gravity. I have found them curled in fetal position, frozen in the final cramps of poisoned agony. I found one impaled on a knife and two more who had sliced their wrists. Sometimes they jump from the cliffs, but this is the worst way to die, for the cliffs are not high and death from exposure and bleeding is slow. None of these were women. Women choose poison. Men will jump. Men will hang. Men will cut. For men, I think, death is violent, a vengeance. For women, death is a release. It is the scolding admonition of a mother, not the blows of a father's fist raised in anger. Men hate. Women love. Men hate, but don't know how to deal with hating. Women, I suspect, have this tender spirit that nurtures to the end, even to the moment of dying. Men despair from hatred and women despair of loving. The end is the same. I have found 70 men and 15 women. The men don't care. Their deaths fairly scream, *I don't care!* The women will dress modestly. They put on their make-up. They will read a favorite poem, eat a little chocolate, listen to a favorite song. Their deaths whisper, *Nobody cared enough.*

It is late afternoon and I lead the way now. The mother and the boy are just about done. Even the father is practically sleepwalking. I stop often and wait for them, scanning the ground for signs, listening, listening, listening. The path here is steep and winding. We scramble over boulders and break through shrubs. Twice I have found threads on branches. Around a bend there is a clearing and the trail forks. I stop.

The family appears. The father fumbles with his GPS. There has been no signal for an hour. The shock of this erased his features. His face is like plastic now.

I hesitate, and he shuffles past me, dutiful wife and son in tow. He looks back.

"Soon it will be dark," I say.

He points his chin up the trail. "It is not far now," he says. "She has to be close."

What he has missed, in his torpor, is the little altar of stone upon which rests an i-phone and a keychain with a little green one-eyed cloth monster. I hold up the little cloth monster and wonder about the things we keep and the things we renounce. *Viveka*. The detachment from things. It is a step on the road to *viraaga*, the letting go of the causes of suffering. They leave altars, the lost souls. And on the altars they place the things they carried with them to the end. I have held so many of these things in my hands—their photographs, rings, journals, books, dried flowers, mementos. The little things to which we attach great meaning. She is near to us. Near to the end, too, I think. I hesitate at the juncture. The path where the family has gone climbs north and west in the direction of her last signal. All day we have traveled north and west.

He trusts technology, this man, this father. He built his life on these modern things. I, on the other hand, cannot. Call me ignorant. Superstitious. All my life I have followed my impulses. I know this is my weakness, but what can I do? The second path leads north and east. It is dark to the west. The afternoon sun warms the cliffs on the eastern face. All my life I have walked in darkness. Which path would I take if I were this girl? I hesitate, then walk towards the light.

It had to happen eventually, she thinks. She's no athlete and she's never walked this far before. Fatigue, dehydration, hunger. It wears you down like ridicule. It saps you from the inside. She was almost to the top when she stumbled and toppled over backwards. The jolt knocked the wind out of her and she lay, for a moment, struggling to comprehend why she couldn't breathe. And then she blacked out. Hunger? Fatigue? The blow? She knows she blacked out—but for how long? She opens her eyes and takes in the quality of the failing light, the short, sharp whistle of a bird unseen in the branches above. The trees here are mountain pines, some tall and straight, others little more than sprawling shrubs sprouting like hope from cracks in the rock. Her neck is sore. Her head, too. She feels her scalp. A cut. Blood on her fingers. She has torn her sweater at the elbow and, on closer examination, finds blood there, too. A gash in the arm. Not deep, not bleeding profusely, but the kind of thing that would burn for a week and leave a scar. She sits up and looks in her bag. She takes out the chocolate bar and the make-up kit. There was still the almond milk, but she doesn't want to drink. The bottle of poison is now a bright, almost glowing, electric green. She draws her knees up under her chin and wraps her arms around herself. It is colder than the night before. How far has she come? Five kilometers? Ten? She stretches her head from side to side and tries to shed the pain. Is waking up from unconsciousness like waking up from death? She looks at the bottle. This doesn't feel like the place, but what difference does it make? No place yet has felt like the place. It's not like the book said at all. There is nothing romantic about it now. It's just another pointless journey, one in a life of endless pointless journeys. She is far from the main trail, perched in a crack in the rock of a cliff now dipped in shadow. She could find her way back if she wanted, and she wishes she did not want to. But she could. Follow the water. Getting here is difficult. Going back is easy. It's downhill. Eventually she'd find the path. But back to what? And what would that make today? Just another failure? Another example of her incompetence? If this is how life is—then to hell with it! She shouts it out loud. "To hell with it!" It felt good to swear. Another rule broken. It was liberating. Empowering. She stood and shouted again, "To HELL with it!" And then she had the strangest feeling that she was not alone.

I had been to this place many times in my youth, but recently, well, perhaps I am becoming lazy. Or old. I walked here as a novice, searching along this precipice for the best view of the valley below and wondering if anyone had ever been here before. Surely someone had been here. And surely someone would wander here again. But still it makes a pretty sight. It opens up so unexpectedly with a vista to the south and west. It is the place where the last sliver of daylight shines down upon the valley. Today there was only a thin line of the orange sun, but still it was fine, so peaceful, and for a moment I stood transfixed, forgetting even why I had come. And then I heard a thud, just a whisper, really, one soft sound in the forest, a little further along the ridge. A falling branch. A rock dislodged. A deer or some other forest creature. I looked at the sun and I looked again, listened for the sound and heard nothing. I looked at the sun, such a fine sight, really, a moment that will pass quickly and then be endlessly repeated, re-incarnated, as it were, each life, each death, different. I was reminded, suddenly, of a story about Milarepa, who had been told by his master to build a house with his own hands, brick-by-brick, stone-by-stone, and when it was done, to tear it down and then start over, to build it again. Every time the master found some flaw in the construction. Tear it down. Build it again. It was an endless cycle of death and rebirth, a constant search for perfection. But perfection, Milarepa would learn, was not found in the building of houses. And if it cannot be accomplished in such a simple thing, then how is it to be attained in the much more difficult task of constructing a life? It is the inner world that matters, Milrepa learned, not the exterior image. That image is the illusion. I could have stood forever in that moment just staring at the sun.

The girl in black has wandered off the path and now climbs slowly up the rocky scree towards the lip of the canyon. In a minute she reaches the top, hauls herself up, stands, stretches, looks around, stares right through me, then shoulders her bag and begins to walk slowly towards the north, straight at me. When she sees me, she stops.

"Hello," I say. I look at the sunset, not the girl. "Isn't it lovely?"

She stands startled.

"I didn't mean to frighten you," I say. "I am sorry. I almost never see anyone here."

She stares at me. "You're from the monastery?"

"Yes. But I'm a failure as a monk."

She looks puzzled. This is, perhaps, not what she was expecting. "Why are you here?" she asks.

It is awkward, this question. "Are you familiar with *viraaga*?" I reply.

She shakes her head.

"I'm tired," I say. "Can we sit? Would you mind? I am old and tired, and it has been a long day."

She sits on a stone and I sit beside her on the ground. We both watch the fading light. "The world is so full of trouble," I say. "It seems there is no end to the suffering. *Viraaga* means renunciation. It means to let go of the suffering of the world. It does not mean not to care about the world, but rather, to detach even from pain. Have you ever felt like that? Like you want to let go of all the pain?"

She nods.

"When I was a boy," I say, "it felt like all I knew was pain." It is almost dark. The forest below melts into the shadow of the hills. I get the feeling she is thinking the same thing that I am thinking. "I used to come up here to disappear. To disappear into the forest. To disappear into the darkness. To disappear from all the pain."

"It must be nice to disappear," she says.

"I don't know," I said. "I think that perhaps we cannot really disappear."

"I think that we can," she says. "I am sure of it."

"That depends," I say. "How you define *disappearance* must depend on how you define *appearance*."

"People think too much about appearance," she says.

"Yes," I say. "I think so too."

"Is that why you became a monk?" she asks.

I think about this. "No," I say. "Maybe. I was always one to ask questions. And I was never satisfied with the answers. My parents —they thought I couldn't do anything right. They said I had no ambition."

She grunts.

Somewhere in the distance an insect chirps, and that moment a half-dozen bats swarm close over us, their wings making a fluttering sound and a breeze. The girl flinches. "There is a cave nearby," I say. "The bats sleep the day in the cave and fly at night." When she looks at me I say, "I've been here before. I've even slept in that cave once. It is quiet and cool."

"We studied bats in school," she says. "But I don't like them."

"My parents—" I begin again. I sigh. "They were denounced in the cultural revolution. They were deemed *zi chan jie ji*. Bourgeois. Their crime was success. They made money. They accumulated property. They were taken away for re-education. They must have known what was coming, for just before they were taken they sent me to stay with an aunt, but she, also, was not well. I pleased her no better than I pleased my parents. In time, I left her and went to live on the streets. This was in Baobing, in Heibei Province, far to the north. I lived on the streets for a long time. I worked as a laborer. I worked in the fields. I kept walking south, village to village. It was warmer in the south. And then one day I came to the monastery. I was twelve or thirteen then, a little old, but they took me anyway. I am not," I say, "a very good monk."

All this time she is sitting with her arms wrapped around her knees. "Why not?" she asks.

"I never had the patience. I hate meditation. I hate the memorization. I didn't like the discipline. It is not easy, being a monk. Much, I suppose, like being in any other school. Do you like school? You do go to school, yes?"

"I hate school," she says. After a moment she adds, "So why did you stay?"

"Where else could I go? I had nothing. And besides, the life of a monk is one of renunciation. I had already done that, after a fashion. *Kaaya-viveka*. It is a life of strict discipline to remove the temptations that cause so much pain. *Kaaya-viveka* is on the path of letting go, but it is an external discipline. It is applied from the outside world and concerns one's dealings with the outside world. There is another path, *citta-viveka,* which means to seek solitude. That also came easy to me. It is easy to run away. Solitude is for contemplation, but the real goal is *upadhi-viveka* . That is what we call *viraaga.*"

The girl looks away. She does not seem the least bit interested, but she turns to me at length and says, "And what is that?"

"*Viraaga* means to let go of the root causes of suffering. To let go on the inside and of the inside."

"I know how that feels," she says.

This surprises me.

She looks around, then fumbles with her pack. She is looking for something.

"*Viraaga* means the renunciation of the attachment to things. Even," I say, "of the feelings we associate with things. This is the real point of Buddhism. Things, you see, cannot make us happy or sad or angry. These feelings arise as part of a mental process. They are actually within our control, though most of us don't see this. It is a thought process, but underlying that process is the way we feel about things. We give these things meaning; we give them power. We think they can help or harm us, but they cannot. Not even the words or actions of another. None of those things have the power at all to hurt us. We generate that hurt."

"But what if somebody hurts us deliberately?"

"Like who?"

"Like . . . someone you love hurts you very much."

"Did this person stick a knife into you?"

"Not exactly, but still . . . "

"Lying?"

"Lying."

"They are only words," I say. "They have no power beyond what I give them."

110

"I don't understand," she says.

I laugh. "Neither do I, really. Perhaps the best I can say is what an old monk once told me. He said: 'We live in a world filled with fools, and we are all fools, all the same, and no one fool is really any better than another. That is the illusion. If there is one thing that might make a difference, it is when I realize that I am not responsible for what other people do or even what they do to me. The only thing I am responsible for is for what I do and for making the world a better place for everybody else. It is only then that one life, more or less, makes any difference.' I am far from perfect—a failure, really—but when I try to do that, it is the only thing that gives meaning to my life. It is the only thing that has ever given meaning to my life."

She smiles. She has a pretty smile. She looks tired.

"My masters used to get so angry with me for my doubting and my questions. As soon as they did I'd say, 'But if detachment is so easy, then why are you angry?' That was why I came to the woods," I say. "I couldn't do anything right. I came to the woods to renounce *renunciation.*"

Her face darkens, and she looks away. When she looks back, she says, "Online it said to be careful of the monk who lives in the woods. Now I know why."

"I can't stop you," I say, "if that's what you really want to do."

"Have you stopped any others?"

"No," I say. "The only ones I have found were gone, or else they had already changed their mind. My job is to tell the families. I bring the authorities to the body and return the things they leave behind."

She is thinking.

I say: "I know what it feels like to want to give up everything. But I also know the difference between a feeling and an action. The Fourth Nobel Truth says that an end to suffering is possible. But it doesn't have to be this end. There are other ways to let go."

When I say this, she begins to cry, softly at first, but then hard, heaving sobs.

"If you will just be patient, little one, you will see that fools and their words wash away like sandcastles in the tide. You have only to wait, walk, let go of what is hurtful, and practice a few simple things. There are people who can help you. Will you come back down with me?" I ask. "It is getting late, and we are far from home."

"My parents sent you," she says.

111

I shake my head.

She looks at me and frown-smiles. "I hear them calling down below."

I listen, but I can't hear them. I must be getting old.

She opens her bag and takes out a bottle, drinks in slow, measured swallows. Then she stops abruptly and looks at me. "Are you thirsty?" she asks.

I nod and she hands me the bottle. In the dark I cannot see what it is, but I drink anyway. Almond milk.

"I have some chocolate, too," she says.

"Chocolate would be good," I say, and she breaks the bar into two pieces.

"How many years have you walked in these woods?" she asks.

I think about this. "Forty years."

"And in all that time you've never stopped anyone?"

I shake my head.

She digs in the bag and takes out another bottle. She unscrews that cap and pours it out.

Now I smile.

When we rejoin her parents there will be hugs all around. They will eat candy bars, drink energy drinks, and find their stride again. They will not wish to spend the night in the forest but will rush back to the monastery. They will light the path with their lights, and I will be the tired one stumbling along behind. They will be embarrassed of the anxiety they displayed this morning. When they reach the monastery they will leave quickly. I'm guessing they have a nice, black, SUV parked in the lot down below.

The prelate will meet me. He will ask what I said and I will tell him, "Nothing." In the dining hall I will find a cloth-covered bowl with some vegetable soup and a plate of rice. Alone in my bunk I will stare at the cracks in the ceiling and feel badly to have lied to her, to all of them. I have, at least once, prevented a suicide. But until this evening it was not any of the other lost souls I have encountered. The men and women who come to the Valley of Shade Trees are masters of their own fate. I haven't lied about that. But when they ask me why I came to these woods so many years ago, that, I suppose, is why I understand them so well. No matter how far I traveled, how long I meditated, how deep into the woods I walked, I carried my pain with me. It was insurmountable and inescapable. It was not enlightenment I sought.

112

My retreat was not renunciation as an act of faith, but rather, the flight of desperation, or even defiance. But somehow, along the way, I lost the courage to do what so many of these have done. Perhaps it was fear that death would not end my suffering. Could one end the cycle of birth, decay, death, and rebirth with a single rash act? I wish it were that easy.

I am a poor monk, and an indifferent traveler in this world. Deep in the forest, fear forced my hand. I could not do anything right. Even that. But tonight I can live with my choice. And perhaps someday, even in a land of a billion people, one person more or less will make a difference. If I could not end my pain, the very least I could do was to help someone else to cope with theirs.

Viveka and *viraaga* are the two Pali words which have been translated as "detachment." The two, however, are not synonymous. The primary meaning of *viveka* is separation, aloofness, seclusion. Physical withdrawal is implied. The later commentarial tradition, however, identifies three forms of *viveka*: *kaaya-viveka* (physical withdrawal), *citta-viveka* (mental withdrawal), and *upadhi-viveka* (withdrawal from the roots of suffering). This last form—*upadhi-viveka*, is also known as *viraaga*.

Superstition

"You must remember something," Kyle said. He's my twelve-year old. He and Katy, my nine-year old, pestered me with questions all the way from Cincinnati.

"Leave your Mama alone," Ray said. Ray's my husband. "It was a long time ago since she left home."

"How long?"

"Lemme see . . ." Ray was never fast at math. "Your mama was eleven, so that makes about . . . twenty-seven years."

Kyle said, "I can remember what I did when I was eleven."

"But that was last year."

"But she must remember something."

I remember going fishing with my brother Zayah. He was maybe, twelve, and I was nine or ten. He fixed me a cane pole with a cork and worm and cast it for me. I could never bring myself to hook the worm. I couldn't stand the way they squirmed. All I could think about was this poor little thing that hadn't done me any harm, and now he was going to die. "It don't hurt the worm none," Zayah said. "They don't feel things like we do." I didn't believe him. I couldn't think about anything but that worm with a hook in him, dying cold and scared, alone in the dark water.

"Why don't you think about something else for a while?" Ray said.

Kyle said, "Like what?"

"Like what you want for a souvenir for to take home."

"I already know what I want."

"What's that?"

South of Atlanta Ray had got tired. The kids were cranky, and we pulled off the interstate for some coffee and something to eat. We found a little roadhouse that served bar-b-cue, and across the road was a fruit stand. Ray couldn't wait to buy peaches, so he and Kyle ran over and came back with a quarter basket. At the produce stand Kyle latched onto some tourists coming back from Florida.

"I want one of those hats," Kyle said.

Ray said, "What hats?"

"You know, one of those hats with the fake doo on it that says 'Damn Seagulls'."

"Listen here," Ray said, his voice rising, "just 'cause some ignorant cracker wants to spend good money to look like a fool don't mean you gots to do it."

"But you axed what I wanted."

"'Nuff foolishness outta you! You keep that talk up, and I'll give you a knock so hard you won't need no hat. We'll paint yo' head red and stick a visor over yo' eyes. And if you want doo, I reckon there's plenty around the farm, right Izzy?"

I nodded, yes. We'd been driving south since supper, passing fields and small towns, patches of piney woods and peach orchards. At that moment we came around a bend and I saw a wide expanse of water, dark and smooth as glass, the last rays of the setting sun reflecting off it like a black mirror. A rocky outcrop stuck out on the far side, and I could see a gap in the hills where the lake drained away in a slow, weed-choked creek that ran down to a cypress swamp.

I remember that lake.

"I remember that lake," I said.

"There now," Ray said, "I told you it would come back."

"I used to fish it with my brother. There was a big catfish, down by the swamp end, but we never caught him. Didn't nobody fish that lake much in those days. There was a superstition said it was haunted."

Katy woke up and rubbed her eyes. She'd been asleep since dinner. "Are we there yet?" she asked.

Ray turned a hopeful eye to me and I nodded. "A mile to go," I said, and I turned towards the window and looked out across the fields.

When I was a little girl there used to be a old bare-boards cabin in that field. I lived in it with Grandma Lizzie and my brother Zayah. I remember inside, the way the morning sun shone through the windows, the glass so old it was opaque, white with age. And I remember an old rockin' chair with a pillow for a seat and a quilt folded over the arm to warm Lizzie's legs. There was a wood-burning cook stove, and a old, squat, pot-bellied black coal-burner Lizzie stoked in the winter. I remember the way the heat used to feel on my skin, and how the smoke used to hang in the rafters. I remember the way it smelled in the morning, with bacon frying, and biscuits—Lizzie used to make her biscuits with lard—and I remember my mouth watering, watchin' 'em rise in the oven. And I remember bein' huddled up in a bed stuffed with feathers she'd plucked herself off the chickens she raised in her yard. She was poor as a old Georgia widow could be, but she had a real featherbed. I'd sink down into that mattress, and the feathers would rise up all around me, and I'd be warm as toast. I couldn't have slept better on a cloud. I didn't know we were poor until I went to the orphanage.

I stared out over the field, but I couldn't see much in the dusk. The house might have fell down by now, but I would have thought the chimney was still standing, unless somebody come along and stole it for the bricks.

"Zayah done pretty good for hisself, didn't he?" Ray asked.

"Yeah" I said. "He done all right." My Ray was born and raised in Cincinnati, so he's a city boy. He wanted to make the trip, and he wanted me to come, but he was still a little fearful about visiting. I think he's cute when he's fussy. He wanted to know all about the farm, whether Zayah had a outhouse, a henhouse, pigs and goats in the yard, what we would eat, where we would sleep. Ray hadn't been south before. All he knew about Georgia came from books and movies, and all I ever heard him say about it was he didn't care much for "crackers."

"Tell me about the haunted lake," Kyle said.

He doesn't miss much. "The Indians told a story about a girl who drowned. They said when the moon was full, and the lake was still, you could see her floating beneath the surface, looking up at the sky. They said if you asked her a question, she could tell you the answer."

"Could she do my homework?"

"Not that kind of question."

"What then?"

"They said she could tell the future or the past."

Ray slowed down and flashed his high beams to see the numbers on the mailboxes. "There it is," he said. He turned into the drive and parked and the porch light came on, and I watched his face relax when he saw that it was just a house like any other. There was a mongrel old shepherd dog barking in the front yard, and Zayah and his missus, Glenda, came to the screen door and waved at us and shouted at the dog to hush up. Kyle and Katy piled out of the car and ran to the steps. Ray turned to me and asked if I was okay.

Am I okay ? I haven't seen my brother since I left home.

116

In the morning I came out on the porch and sat on the steps with a cup of coffee. The dog came out of the field, jumping a low spot in the fence. He had mud on his face and paws. He looked like a dog what had been up to no good. He shook the dew off his back and gave me a innocent look, then a hopeful look, but when I didn't have nothing to feed him he got disinterested and trotted around the house to the back yard. Glenda was frying bacon and baking biscuits in the house; the smell was heavenly. Kyle was inside pesterin' Zayah about the lake.

"Mama says there's monster catfish in there."

"Tha's right," Zayah said. I had forgotten how sweet his voice was.

"You gots to sit still, Izzy, 'cause them fish can see better than anything. And you gots to be quiet, too, 'cause they can hear."

"How can they hear when they ain't got no ears?" I asked.

Zayah plunked his line in the water and grinned at me. "Kin you hear when you sticks your head in the tub?"

"'Course I can."

"Well, so can the fish, only, since they underwater all the time, they got their ears on the inside so they don't fill up with water. They hear good, too."

"Can they hear us talkin'?"

"I reckon. They can hear the bees buzzing, and the flies humming, and when we throw a line in the water, they can hear that, too. That's how they eat. When a fish hear something fall in the water, he thinkin', 'tha's my dinner.' So you gots to be quiet when you fish, otherwise we won't catch no supper."

We watched our corks bobbin' in the water, and then I forgot all about being quiet. I said "Bomby Sosher said he saw a stranger camped out in the cypress swamp last week."

Zayah looked at me and bit his lip. "Bomby's skeered of his shadow," he said. "He ain't seen nothing over in the swamp. He don' even go in the swamp. What was he doin' in the swamp, anyway?"

"His mammy sent him over to see if the mayhaws is ripe yet."

"Well, I reckon he's just trying to skeer folks off so he can keep all the mayhaws for hisself."

"I bet he ain't. He was so skeered he 'lowed his mammy couldn't wup him hard 'nuff to make him go back."

"Shoot," Zayah said. "How'd he know it was a stranger?"

"'Cause he hadn't seen him 'round before."

"And how'd he know he was campin' in the woods?"

"'Cause he said he walked into his camp and there wasn't nobody around, and he kinda looked around a little bit, and all of a sudden he looked up and seed this man a walkin' towards him."

"What'd he look like?"

"Bomby said he was tall and scrawny and had wild hair and hadn' shaved and looked like he'd been sleeping in the woods for a while."

"Did he say anything?"

"Bomby said he didn' stick aroun' to find out. He dropped everything an' run."

Zayah's cork bobbed once, twice, then it went under, and Zayah gripped his pole to set the hook. But then the cork come back up, and we saw that big cat roll over in the water, real slow. "He laughin' at us," Zayah said, and he pulled his hook outta the water and saw that the worm was gone. "Come on, we might as well go home. We won' catch 'im today."

When I was a little girl that seemed like the longest mile, from the lake to the cabin. The road wasn't paved, it was just old red Georgia clay, and we were barefoot, hot and thirsty. I remember the way the clay squished between my toes when it was rainin' and how hard the ground was in summer when it was dry—or winter when it was cold. I remember the way the little stones felt under my heel and watching out for stickers. I knew when we got home we wouldn't have nothin' but bread and gravy for supper with maybe some peas or green corn. That was the longest walk, the walk home from the lake.

I said to Zayah, "I'm sorry for spoiling yo' fishin'."

"Tha's all right," he said, and he put his arm around me while we walked. Then he stopped and looked at me real serious and said, "Izzie, don't you be talkin' to no strangers you see around here, you unnerstan'? If you see a stranger in the woods you run away. You run home jus' as fas' as you can, you hear?"

* * * * *

Ray came out on the porch with his plate piled high with bacon and eggs and grits and biscuits. The smell set my mouth watering. He took a deep breath and said something about how good it felt to be out of the city. It would get hot in the afternoon, but the morning air was crisp and felt good on my skin. The air was clean and the sun was bright—it sparkled off the dew on the grass in the yard. The air tasted good. There wasn't a freeway or factory for miles. It was quiet, too. Glenda asked if I wanted to come to the table, but I said I'd just sit on the steps for a bit, so she brung me my breakfast. A few minutes later, Zayah came out and sat down beside me, then Kyle and Katy, and finally Glenda, too, though she grumbled about not eating at the table like proper folks.

"Uncle Zayah's gonna take me fishing," Kyle said.

Katy said, "Me too. I'm gonna catch a catfish!"

Zayah's a good-looking man, with thick lips and big hands, almost always a smile on his face. He's tall and strong. I remember him as skinny—he was all arms and legs as a boy. His hair used to be thick and curly, but he's gone bald early, and what hair he has left is about half-gray. He's got a big bald spot right on the top of his head, shiny as a bowling ball. He looks like a Irish monk. I started giggling, and Zayah asked me what I was thinking and I said, "You look like a Irish monk."

"Humph!" Zayah said. "Ain't no Irish in me."

When he called I nearly fell off my chair. "How did you find me?" I asked.

Ray came home and found me cryin'. He's always been good to me, Ray has. He knows how scared I get when we visit his folks. He always holds my hand and stays real close. He never asked too many questions. When I told him I couldn't remember he looked at me and nodded. It was enough for Ray that I told him the truth.

"It don't matter," Zayah said. "I foun' you. Tha's what matters."

When Zayah asked if we could get together, Ray put his arm around me and said, "Maybe it's time you found out."

* * * * *

"Why'd you come back?" I asked. I set my plate on the step and looked at Zayah. "Why here?"

"I dunno. I guess it's all the home I got." He slurped his coffee and thought for a while. "I think I was waiting for you."

"What happened to the old place?"

"I heard some kids burned it down. When I come back, there wasn't even a bare spot. It was all growed over. Some cracker even hauled off the bricks and the stoves."

* * * * *

I remember in the winter I'd scruntch up under the covers and wait for Lizzy to get up and light the fire. Grandma Lizzy would git up, grumbling about her arther-itis, and I'd hear her stump across the floor in her socks and come back from the coal bin with a few lumps for the fire. I remember the screech the grate made when she swung it open and Lizzy poking at the ashes to rake the coals in a pile. There would be frost on the inside of the windows of the house like rock candy, and Zayah once told me it was rock candy, and I froze my tongue to the glass tasting it to see if it was true. Lizzy had to pour warm water on my tongue to get it un-stuck, and Zayah had to fetch hisself a switch and then take a licking with it.

Lizzy would build a fire and put on a pot of coffee and maybe some grits to boil, and when it warmed up a bit me and Zayah would get up and race to go roust the chickens and see if we had any eggs for breakfast. We always claimed the eggs we found for ourselves, and Grandma Lizzy always said she fixed 'em for us like that, but how she scrammeled 'em in the skillet and kept 'em separate I never knew.

I remember one morning watching the sun melt the frost off the windows, and Zayah was out in the garden diggin' worms to fish, and I crawled into Lizzy's lap and asked her to tell me about my mama.

Lizzy was a jet-black, blue-gum African woman, wide as a church door, her lap big an' sof' as the bottom forty. She'd worked her whole life as a field hand and a cook, and she didn't have nothing to show for it but bad knees and a achin' back. When my mama died, Lizzy took me and Zayah in and did the best she could. She gleaned fields. She took in sewing. She drew a little pension from a church, and sometimes the church folk would bring her a basket of food or some coal. She kept chickens and a milk goat in the yard, and me and Zayah kept her in fish most of the summer, when we wasn't in school.

Lizzy eased herself down into her rockin' chair and took me up in her arms. "Yo' mama," she said, "was the beautifulest wom'n that eve' liv'. The sun always shine' on her and the wind was jealous on

120

account of how graceful and pretty she walked. And when she used to sing . . . well all the church folks knew that God heared they prayers 'cause when yo' mama sang, even God stopped what he was doin' an' listen'."

* * * * *

Kyle and Katy come around the side of the house with a shovel and a bucket, the mongrel dog in tow. "Where do we dig for worms?" they asked Zayah.

Zayah shoved the last biscuit into his mouth and handed his plate to me. "Come on," he said, and he took the kids back around the house. Glenda poured me some more coffee and took the plates. Ray came back whistling down the road and sat down beside me. Across the highway an old farmer in a tractor pulled a flatbed out into a field of watermelons.

"I remember picking watermelons," I said. "I got a dollar a day and a melon to take home. 'Course, me and Zayah used to sell our melons alongside the highway. We could always sneak back at night and get more, so long as Grandma Lizzy didn't find out."

Zayah, Kyle, Katy and the dog came around side of the house with a bucket of dirt and three cane poles. Katy ran up and opened her hand for me to see. A fat night crawler wriggled on her palm. "I found this one myself," she said. "Uncle Zayah says it'll catch fish, for sure."

"Is he going to put it on the hook for you?" I asked. She is my sensitive child; she can't stand to see something hurt.

"I can do it," she said. "Uncle Zayah says it doesn't hurt them. You want to come along?"

"I don't think so," I said.

Zayah said, "We're going to the lake."

"You ever go back to Mooseman's Pond?" I asked.

"Bunch of rich white folks from Albany bought all that land. Developed it. It's private now. I heard they got it stocked with bass, but they got a gate up, and they don't let no colored folks in, 'cept to cut the grass and clean they houses."

* * * * *

Mooseman's always was the white folks' pond. I remember walking over with Zayah and findin' a bunch of white boys fishing

121

there, and them tellin' us we couldn't fish it. Zayah said that was okay with him, but if they didn't mind, he'd just rest a while and watch, seein' as how we'd done walked so far and it was so hot out.

Them white boys said they didn' mind us watchin' so long as we was quiet and didn't stay. So we sat down with our backs against a willow tree, and after a while Zayah says, "What ya'll fishin' with, anyhow?"

One of the white boys answered, "What's it to you, nigger?"

Zayah said, "It's nothin' to me. I jus' don't see you catchin' anythin', and I wondered what you was fishin' with, that's all."

So the white boy says, "Red worms," and Zayah kinda nodded his head. Then them white boys get to looking kinda antsy, and findly one of 'em says, "Look here, nigger, you see sompthin' funny?"

And Zayah says, "No, sir. I shore don'. I was just thinkin' to myself how las week, down at Miller's Store, I heard this pond was all fished out of fish what eats red worms, and everybody knows ol' man Miller knows more 'bout fishin' than anybody else hereabouts. And I was just thinkin' that if I shared my nightcrawlers with you, you might catch some fish, 'specially since these here is special nightcrawlers, and seein' as how they gots to die anyhow, on account of I dug 'em up en all. But ya'll probably don' want no nightcrawlers what a nigger brung, anyhow."

"See here, nigger," says the white boys, "what's so special about yo' worms anyhow that you think they kin catch fish when our'n can't."

And Zayah says, "I raised these worms myself in a pile of ol' horse manure. It's a powerful bad smellin' ol' pile, and a heap of trouble to keep, but the worms is the bes'. They strong, and the ol' fish can't seem to leave 'em alone. But I reckon' you boys don' want my worms, so I'll jus throw 'em out by the road on the way home and let the birds have 'em."

The white boys looked from one to the other and talked kinda low among theirselves. Then one of 'em says, "Ain't no sense throwin' out good worms, nigger. You give us your worms and we'll give 'em a fair try."

"Suppose," Zayah said, "I give you half my worms. You s'pose me and my sister could fish over there on to the other side of the pond, over by that oak what hangs out over the bullrushes?"

The white boys huddled up fo' a minute, then one of 'em up and sez, "S'pose you give us all your worms, and we give you wat's lef o' our'n, and then you kin go fish over to the other side of the pond."

Zayah kinna himmed and hawed and drew in the dirt with his finger. Then he got up and traded worms with the white boys, and we *walked around to the other side of the pond. Zayah opened up his tackle box and he took out a ball of what looked like clay and started to break it up. "What you got there, Zayah?" I asked.*

"I got a piece of cheese I kept buried in a clay bank. Old man Miller tol' me once that if the fish ain't bitin' worms, try some ripe cheese on 'em." So I set this aside for jus' such a occasion. 'Sides," he added, "this time 'o day, all the fish are goin' to be hidin' in the bullrushes where it's cool."

Zayah and me caught a string of bluegill that afternoon while the white boys watched us and jus' steamed. We traded some at a farmhouse down the road for a peck of new peas, and we ate all we wanted for dinner.

* * * * *

Glenda came out on the porch wiping her hands on her apron. "You okay, hun?" she asked.

"I'm all right," I replied, but I had my knees drawn up to my chin and my hands clenched so tight my nails left marks in the skin.

She sat down on the step next to me. "Is it what you expected?"

I don't know what I expected. I said, "Things change, I suppose."

"Zayah sure does love you."

"I know."

"He looked awful hard to find you."

"I know."

"He said that when they took you, it like to broke his heart."

When they took you.

"You don't remember, do you?"

I shook my head.

"It'll come back." Glenda patted me on the arm. "Just give it time."

I said, "I think I'll go for a walk."

* * * * *

Zayah told me the church burnt down, the old whitewashed frame building we prayed and sang in when I was a little girl. I remember standin' there and the steeple looked as high as the moon.

Bomby Sosher said he climbed up it once, but Bomby Sosher said a lot of things. The Mt. Zion Baptists built another one out of brick in the same place.

Zayah said he was on the building committee. He wasn't much for church when he was a boy, but he said Glenda got him right with the Lord. He don't drink. He don't smoke. I never heard him cuss. He and Glenda raised two girls, and as far as I heard they were straight as an arrow. They both go to college in Louisiana. Church is their life, just like it was Lizzy's.

I remember hearing that Lizzy was so old, her parents had been born slaves. She must have had children besides mom, but I don't remember them. Maybe she was my great-grandmother, I don't know.

It was hot and I forgot to bring water. I found a spigot outside the church and drank from the tap. I splashed water on my face and wiped the perspiration away. A truck roared down the highway on the other side of the fields. I looked back and watched the afternoon heat rise in shimmering waves. A covey of quail burst from the field, the beat of their wings, their sharp cries breaking the afternoon stillness.

We were gathered around a grave. There was no coffin, but they had turned the earth just the same and put up a headstone. The deacon was preachin', but the strangest thing was that the choir couldn't bring themselves to sing.

I wished I had brought flowers. I meant to pick some along the way, but I forgot, and there are none to be seen around the church. I look at the names on the headstones. Lizzie. Rachel. There is no last name. How can a person live and die in America with no last name? The stones are green with moss. I kneel on the grass. It feels cool on my knees. I brush the moss away from the names. The stone crumbles. The edges are rounding out. In a few years the names won't be readable. The moss stains the tips of my fingers green, and it reminds me of rotting flesh.

After the funeral I asked Lizzie, "Tell me about my daddy."

That night she held me in her arms and rocked me to sleep, her big hands brushing the hair away from my eyes. I remember the scratchy feeling the calluses on the tips of her fingers left when they touched my face, the way her skin hung slack under her arms, and how she smelled like an old woman. But it was a good smell, earthy, like smoke, and moss, and crumbling stone. I remember Zayah, all arms and legs, huddled up on the bed with his eyes as big as the moon. "Tell me about my daddy," I said.

Lizzy said, "Did you evah hear da story 'bout Romeo and Juliet?"

I shook my head, no.

"Well, they was white folks, but some things is the same. Romeo and Juliet lived far away in some kinna castle or somepin'. And Romeo was from one fambly, and Juliet was from anotha, and they famblies couldn't get along. They was always fightin', and wheneber the one fambly would see da otha one, dey would go for dey swords and have a big set-to. But Romeo was a boy, and Juliet was a girl, and dey met at the market or somethin', an' they fell in love. But when dey foun' out dey couldn' be together, it was jus' too much for dem to bear, so Romeo ran off an' joint da army and neva saw Juliet ag'in."

Across the field I heard Kyle and Katy shouting. They were walking with Ray and Zayah. They had all caught fish.

* * * * *

Glenda herded us to the table that evening, and we stuffed ourselves on catfish and hush puppies, turnip greens, and sweet potato pie. We sat over coffee long after the children went to bed.

"You s'pose he's still alive," I asked.

Zayah set his cup down and looked at me.

"The catfish, I mean."

"I reckon," Zayah said. "They live a long time."

Zayah was always gonna catch that fish. I remember him standing in the doorway with our cane poles, Lizzy pushing me out of her lap and shooing us out of the house. "Don' ya'll be foolin' aroun' wid dat catfish. Ya'll gwine over to Mooseman's and brin' back a mess of crappie, you hear?"

Me and Zayah started out, but when we reached the fork in the road to Mooseman's, Zayah kept on walkin'. "Ain't we goin' over to Mooseman's," I asked.

"No," Zayah said. "I reckon I'll catch that big cat this mornin'."

"If Lizzy finds out, she'll wup our hides."

"But I guess if I catch that big cat, we'll have fish enough to smoke, an' then she won' mind, now will she?"

"I reckon not. But suppose you don't catch that cat, and somebody was to see us and tell where we'd been?"

"Well, if you scared to come, then you go on over to Mooseman's, and I'll catch up wid you by-'n-by. Just don't fall in. Now I gots to go catch me that big cat, so you run along, an' I'll see you in a hour or so."

The sun was shining, and it was warm. I knew the way. I had been there lots of times before, and I didn't think nothin' of walking by myself. I'm sure I had walked alone some time or another, to see a friend or whatever. So that morning Zayah took the left fork in the road, and I took the right. I was listening to the meadowlarks sing, and watching the butterflies, and thinking to myself, maybe singing a little girl song, and after a while I come up over a little rise in the road and ran into a man I hadn't seen before.

He was tall, and his hair was long and brown, and he hadn't shaved. He looked like he'd been sleeping out in the woods. His shirt had the sleeves cut off. His arms was scrawny, strong like a kudzu vine, and covered with pictures. I remember a blue eagle, and a naked woman, and another one of a knife through a heart dripping blood. I remember all this 'cause I saw it real good and close.

I got up from the table. "I'm going for a walk," I said.

Ray paused, a fork full of pie in his hand. "I'll come with you," he said.

I said, "I want to be alone." I stopped outside and leaned against the car. My breath came in gasps. I thought for a minute I might hyperventilate. I almost went back, but then I heard Ray and Zayah and Glenda talking in the kitchen over the clatter of the dishes.

Glenda said, "She's been like this all day."

Ray said, "She's been like this since you called."

* * * * *

A quarter mile this side of the lake was a fork in the road with a big iron-gate I didn't remember. The road, that used to be clay, was now asphalt. Over the rise I knew there were rich people's houses,

126

maybe a golf course, and Mooseman's Pond, stocked with bass for the white folks to catch. I figured the woods had been cleared of underbrush, and I pictured in my mind elegant young girls from private schools cantering horses along shaded paths, maybe a jogger or two out running for their health.

I remember flying down that road as fast as my bare feet would carry me. I remember everything about that morning, the pale blue dress I wore, a little silver chain my mother left me rattling around my neck. I screamed for Zayah and he came running across the fields up from the lake. He gathered me in his arms and I wrapped myself around him, buried my face in his chest and cried.

"Izzy," he said, "did you get bit by a snake?" and I said "No."

"Then wha's the matter?"

After a while I stopped sobbing long enough to tell him, "I met the stranger that Bomby Sosher saw."

"How did that stranger look?" Zayah asked.

"He looked just like Bomby Socher said. He was wild and his hair and beard was growed out, and he had him a pack, and he looked like he'd been sleeping in the woods."

"Did that stranger say anything to you?"

I tried to remember what the stranger said. "He said he wanted to give me something."

"Did he touch you?"

I looked down at my feet and started to cry. "He helt me in his arms," I said, "an run his fingers thru my hair, and he tol' me over an' over how pretty I was."

I looked at the gate and it was tall and wrought iron. It opened with a motor by remote control, but it wasn't nothing but a gate, and I had no trouble climbing it.

Zayah carried me down to the lake where he left his things. He opened his tackle box and stuck his filletin' knife through the loop on his coveralls. He hid the box and his pole in the bushes, and we started back up the road to Mooseman's Pond. We come over the rise and I showed him the place by the side of the road where I had thrown away my fishin' pole. The stranger was gone.

We walked on to the pond, and them same white boys was fishin', and they waved to us and asked us if we heard about one-eyed Jake Palmer. Zayah said he hadn't, but he wanted to know if the white boys had seen a stranger around. The white boys said they hadn't, but if we did we should call the po-lice, because they heard a stranger took a fire poker to Jake's head that morning and kilt him. They said the police had heard there was a stranger about town askin' for Jake, and they reckoned it was him what did it.

Zayah and me headed home, but before we got over the rise we heard dogs, and then a black and white come down the road and the police got out and asked Zayah if we'd seen anybody.

I shook my head, "No," but Zayah jerked me by the arm, and I saw the police kinda look at each other side-a-ways. Then one of 'em came and scrunched down in front of me and said, "Look-a-here little girl, if you seen something, you best tell us now, ya' hear? 'Cause this here man we're lookin' for done kilt a white man, and he's in some baaaad trouble."

I didn't say nothin', but Zayah said, "She saw this here stranger what's been hangin' around, but he skeered her up something awful. I kin show you the spot, if you like."

One of the police jumped in the car and grabbed the radio, and the other took me by the hand, and Zayah walked ahead of us up to the clearing by the side of the road. He hunted around in the grass for a little while, and after a while he bent down and held up two silver dollars. "Well," he said, "will you look at that." He put the money in his pocket.

A few minutes later another police car came, and a truck with a couple of fellas with hound dogs and rifles. They turned the dogs loose, and in a minute they took to bayin' and hollerin', and they took off at a trot, with the police close behind. Zayah and me walked home. Wasn't long before we heard a shot in the woods.

I laid down on my back in the grass by the side of the road and watched the full moon rise until it was high in the sky. I heard Ray and Zayah in the distance calling my name, but I didn't answer, and they didn't come. After a while I got up.

When I was a little girl Grandma Lizzy used to tell me that the Indians said the lake was haunted and they wouldn't fish there. She said they told a story about a maiden who lost her lover and drowned herself. And when the moon was full, and the lake was smooth as black glass, she said you could look down in the water and see her there, and she will tell you your past or your future.

I walked to the lake, and then around to the far side, climbed out on the rock and looked down into the depths, and the moon was reflected off the water. Off in the trees I could hear an owl hoot, and its

128

mate reply from swamps behind me. I heard the splash of a frog startled into jumping, and then everything went quiet. The heat faded, and I felt the dew settle onto the rock. I heard the trees, the grass, the lily pads, the bulrushes rustling in the shallow part of the lake. I took a chill. And then I saw the shadow in the water below, reaching up to touch my face. Her body was thin and her eyes glittered. Her dark hair fanned out around her shoulders like a black halo, and I knew she was not an Indian. It was my mother who haunted that lake. I looked down and asked her my past, and she told me the story of Romeo and Juliet.

Once upon a time there was a white boy who lived on a farm and a black girl who lived in a cabin across the road, and they grew up together, and played together, and they didn't think anything about it. And the white boy loved the black girl, but their families had been feuding for a long time, and so they couldn't be together. But some folks knew about it anyway, and you know how people like to talk. And they made it hard on the white boy and the black girl. After a while there was a war, and the white boy joined the army to fight in Korea. And Romeo never knew Juliet was with child.

While Romeo was gone, some other white boys caught Juliet walking down the road, and they had heard how she had loved a white boy before, so they grabbed her and dragged her into the woods. And when they were done she was with child again. And she wanted to press charges, but nobody cared because, after all, since she had loved one white boy, she might as well love them all.

And when Romeo came home from the war and found out what happened, he beat one boy half to death, put his eye out. The judge sent Romeo to prison. And while Romeo was in jail the boy who lost his eye came back and killed Juliet. He wrapped her body in chain and threw it in the lake, and even though the police dragged the lake they couldn't find nothing', and without a body they couldn't charge him with murder, so he went free. They used to have a saying about it, "Just like a nigger to steal more chain than she could swim with."

When Romeo got out of prison he came home and found the man who killed Juliet. He beat him to death with a fire poker. And on his way out of town he met a little girl on the road. This girl was not quite his daughter, but was the child of the woman he loved. Romeo wanted to tell the little girl how much he loved her mother, but the little girl was scared, she didn't know who he was. And the man said he wanted to give the little girl something, the only thing he had left in the world—two silver dollars—and he pressed the money into her

hand and then gathered her in his arms and held her. But the little
girl screamed, and when the stranger dropped her, she ran away.

I remember the man with the scrawny arms wrapped around
me, the tattoos, the smell of campfire smoke in his hair, the wild look
in his eye, desperate as a treed coon. "You are as beautiful as your
mother," he said. There was dried blood on his coveralls.

Sometime, alone in the dark night, that old catfish turned over
on the water and looked at me. His back was black and shiny as a
beautiful woman, but when he rolled I could see his belly, white as a
white man. He is mixed, mixed up like me, and I wonder if I will ever
be whole again.

There is a moon above and a moon below and a thin column of
white light flowing in between. The ripples on the lake rise and seem to
me as high and inaccessible as the distant mountains of Asia. They are
lines of black and white rolling in the moonlit night. In a mirror world
beneath the water my mother presses her dead fingers against the sky
and waits for her lover to return. I reach my fingers towards hers and
the shock of cold water breaks the spell. I watch for a moment,
confused about what I see. And then I whisper in a little girl's voice,
"Mama, it's me, remember . . ."

Harijan

The mattress is of coconut husks—the cheapest and poorest mattress the world has ever seen. It's a poor man's mattress, the husks not even broken into fiber, just stuffed into a hand-stitched oversized burlap sack. The locals say that coconut husk mattresses support the posture, that the coconut itself has cooling properties, and that, at the very least, it discourages bedbugs. *And sleep,* Father Juricich sometimes adds on the nights when he lies on his back, the husks digging into it and aggravating his old war wounds. *And sleep.*

It's two a.m., the hottest part of the day, and Father Juricich should be napping, but a myriad of distractions keep him at the brink of, but unable to slip over the edge into, sleep. At first, it was the mattress. Then it was the ceiling fan rattling and grinding as it stirred the desultory air of his room. Then it was the obsessive notion that the fan was about to come unfastened and fall onto the bed below—not an impossibility given the age of the fan and the condition of the ceiling. He got up and shut off the fan but the room grew hot. He kicked off the covers. He rolled over. He rolled back. He turned the fan back on and pulled the covers to his chin. Finally he relaxed. He tricked his mind into allowing the sound to more or less hypnotize him. The drowsiness he craved melted into his consciousness like a teabag seeping into warm milk. And then Father Juricich felt the sting of an insect, and thereafter his skin was hyper-sensitized. He felt like he was being eaten alive. Finally, he prayed, mindful of his human frailty, and of the suffering of the martyred saints before him who had undergone infinitely worse, and Father Juricich offered himself as a living sacrifice to every hungry mosquito and biting fly passing through the neighborhood. Then he gave up.

At length he sighed, eased out of his bed, and slipped into his black kurta—he had long ago abandoned the official priestly garb in favor of an Indian/western hybrid. He checked his watch and smoothed the pages of the diary on his desk, but before he began to write he opened his bedroom door and looked in the front room for Shunita, his housekeeper. She was gone, to market, napping, doing the laundry, something. So Father Juricich lit the burner on the little gas stove and made his own coffee, grinding the beans in a hand-cranked mill mounted on the wall, then boiling the grounds in sweetened milk and straining them out of the finished coffee through a cheesecloth. But before he could drink, there was a knock at the door.

Two boys stood on the steps outside, wheezing and panting, having run, apparently, for some distance. It took Father Juricich a moment to recognize them. They were from the Nair family, a large clan of devout Hindus. They were not on the list of regular callers the priest might have expected.

"Come, come!" one boy shouted. And the other echoed, "Come, quick! There has been *accident!*" He placed extra emphasis on the final word.

Father Juricich looked at the sun beating straight down on his garden. He prayed inwardly that he wouldn't have to walk far but knew intuitively that he would. He scolded himself for his self-indulgence. "Just a moment," he said. He partially closed the door and went into his room, slipped on his sandals, made a mental note to take a bottle of water, found his old, well-worn, traveling Bible, and then left, forgetting the water.

Neither of the boys spoke good English, and when Father Juricich inquired in his broken Malayalam what was the matter, they jabbered excitedly, and Father Juricich couldn't make heads or tails of what they said. They took him by the hands and rushed him along, and Father Juricich tried to oblige, forcing his long legs to make up in length-of-stride what he lacked in foot speed. He wondered what catastrophe might have brought the Nair boys to his door, with the most likely scenarios being that some foreigner had OD'd or become ill or suffered misfortune in one of the city's back alleys, or that a dispute flared between Hindus and Muslims over a business deal gone bad, or a son and daughter caught in indecency, or some other such rubbish that might call for a neutral adjudicator.

Whatever the problem, Father Juricich was sure it would have nothing to do with the ministry. Thirty-eight years as a Jesuit evangelist in India had taught him one thing: he was an absolute failure. Father Juricich did not know for what purpose the good Lord had led him to India, but he was certain that, whatever it was, it had nothing to do with saving souls.

* * * * *

Francis Xavier Juricich was the seventh son of a Polish coalminer, his father the seventh son of a Polish coalminer (though his mother traced her roots to Scottish immigrants to Poland in the 1880's). He got his broad shoulders, thick neck, and round head from his father; his red hair and hot temper from his mother. He might have tunneled happily under Poland his whole life had it not been for the rise of Nazi Germany.

His mother had hoped from the beginning that Francis Xavier would become a priest—as evidenced by his christening—and in 1938, with the rumor of war casting a pall over Poland, she sent Francis to stay "for just a little while" with distant relatives in Scotland. For a time he attended a remedial school for refugees run by the Jesuits, but as soon as he turned eighteen he enlisted in the British Army. He was assigned to a transport battalion and drove a truck for Montgomery in North Africa until it struck a mine and injured his spine. He was not certain if this was bad luck or good. A bad back is nothing to hope for, but it secured him a medal, an honorable discharge, and British citizenship by virtue of his war-wounds. It also dimmed considerably his long-term prospects for future employment. And with the pain, and the anxiety that came with the pain, came the insomnia that would plague Francis Xavier for the rest of his life.

He recuperated four months at an Army hospital in Alexandria, Egypt, then sailed for England in the fall. But the ship was torpedoed off the coast of Ireland. Five hundred and fifty-six men drowned that night. Seventeen survived.

Francis Xavier Francis took his discharge in Ireland and applied for work at a number of jobs, but the condition of his back made him unfit for manual labor, even driving, and his poor English made him unsuitable for clerical work. He fumbled along from job to job, able to make do primarily because of the manpower shortage. But his luck ran out when the war ended and the troops came home. In the summer of 1947 he applied, reluctantly, to enter the Jesuit Order.

He was interviewed twice by priests and examined three times by physicians. At one of the meetings, a priest asked Francis how strong was his faith. Francis replied that he believed in God, but found the issue of faith and calling confusing. The truth was, he didn't really know. He left the interview dejected and was surprised two weeks later to receive a letter advising him that he had been admitted as a novice. Francis entered the seminary feeling somewhat like Job, vomited onto the shore from which he had fled.

* * * * *

Rahul Nair was nearly eighty, a staunch Malayalam Nationalist and a Hindu, well-respected in the community for both his business acumen and his charitable works. He was one of the first to invite Father Juricich into his home, in 1965, when Father Juricich arrived in India. They were not close, but had kept up a cordial relationship. The Nair family, more than sixty in all, not counting servants, lived in a large, walled compound on the eastern side of the highway, beyond the commercial district and the railroad tracks. Father Juricich's nightly ministry sometimes took him past the Nair home. It was more impressive in the dark. The daylight revealed the urine-stained outer walls (once painted white), the crumbling stucco of the building façade, the neglected grounds, the blue plastic tarps stretched and tied and weighted down with stones to cover the leaking roof, the accumulation of junk bricks and cars and spare parts along the side of the house.

The Nair's had bought the compound in 1947 from a British government official pulling out in anticipation of Indian independence. Nothing had been done with the place since. That would have been the year Father Juricich passed from Novice to Formed Scholastic, though Father Juricich remembered it more as the year a young Red Cross volunteer came to his door and told him flatly that all of his Polish family had died in concentration camps—the price, the volunteer sympathized, of loyal resistance. If his mother's intuition about the Nazi's had been right, it was small consolation at the time.

The wrought iron gate at the main entry stood open. The driveway was crammed with cars and motorcycles. The boys hurried Father Juricich through the front door. Inside, a number of grim-faced Nairs, all male, clutched cups of coffee or chai and occupied every available chair in the parlor, then spilled out into the hallway where they leaned against the walls in tight-lipped silence. There were candles lighted on every table and shelf in sight. The boys left Father Juricich in the entry. Several of the Nairs nodded but none addressed him. A moment later the boys returned with Naresh Nair, Rahul's oldest son. He led Father Juricich upstairs to the master bedroom.

Rahul lay in bed attended by his wife and sisters. Dr. Bondre, a well-known local Ayurvedic physician, was concluding an examination. In one corner the family had set up a table with a statue of Shiva. The image was garlanded with yellow flowers and surrounded by small candles. A stick of incense filled the room—a fragrance both salty and sweet. Dr. Bondre sorted out a container of pills with Mrs. Nair and left several bottles of oil on the dresser by the bed.

It was clear to Father Juricich what happened: Rahul had suffered a stroke. The old man was dressed in plain, white pajamas, his arms folded on his stomach, the covers pulled up to his chest. His white hair and flowing moustache had been combed. His right eye was closed, a single spot of moisture glistened under the lid. The right side of Rahul's face sagged and his lips and chin hung slack. But his left eye was open wide, and Rahul watched Father Juricich. With his left hand Rahul gestured for Father Juricich to come closer. Father Juricich bent his ear to Rahul, and Rahul whispered, "Priest, I need you to make a miracle."

Father Juricich squirmed. He wasn't sure what to make of Rahul's request. On the other side of the bed he locked eyes with Naresh. Naresh was dark-complected with obsidian eyes and a thick black moustache. Despite the fact that he was over fifty, he was still a formidable man, nearly six feet tall and muscular. He was the Kannur District Secretary for the CPM, the Communist Party of Kerala, and he frequently made religion—any religion—an object of scorn in his speeches.

Mrs. Nair and Mr. Nair's sisters huddled against the far wall. They were Hindus. Mrs. Nair had once made a barefoot pilgrimage to the top of a snow-covered mountain to prove her devotion. They had shown Father Juricich pictures of the trek. But that was a long time ago. Even then, when she was nearing forty, she was beautiful; beautiful in the way of those Indian women who eat well, practice yoga, and dress in fine silk saris.

It was hard, Father Juricich thought, to be a woman in India. She is raised from infancy to be given away, often with a bribe-like dowry as an incentive for the groom's family to accept her. And once given away she drifts like Ruth following Naomi into the house of strangers. But in this home, Mrs. Nair reigned supreme, a rare triumph, and one deserving respect. She raised three sons and two daughters, buried one of each. One daughter died of Typhoid at seventeen. One son died was burned alive by anti CPM activists who mistook him for his father. One daughter was married to an official of the Southern Railways and made her home in Trivandrum. The other son was a dentist who had left India many years ago to live in America.

135

Father Juricich thought he was the least likely priest on earth to perform a miracle. Privately he still wasn't sure he believed in God, not, at least, in the proper Catholic sense of the word. He had believed, for a time, after he joined the seminary. But during the eleven years between his acceptance as a Formed Scholastic and his ordination as a Professed Jesuit, time spent in study, meditation, practical ministry, Father Juricich had become enamored of a curiously Buddhist point in Jesuit doctrine. This initially small crack had widened into a yawning maw which Father Juricich found increasingly difficult to straddle. The point was this: that the truth of all faith was Love, inspired by Wisdom, interpreted in the Spirit of Charity. And though there was an ultimate authority, the General of the Order, who resided in Rome and answered to the Pope, there was a great deal of room for interpretation within the order as to how to express this love, so that despite its roots in the crusades, the Jesuits today could yield activists in a variety of flavors: from revolutionary priests in Mexico, South America, Africa, and Ireland; to militant peace activists in Asia and the United States. Father Juricich had worked with members of both factions and found it difficult to envision them as operating under the same vow and in the same cloth. Could resistance and reconciliation both be expressions of love?

But the Jesuits themselves had no problem with this dichotomy, and since "once a priest, always a priest," one could run afoul of doctrine and be expelled but know he would be taken back if he asked. This Father Juricich knew all-too-well. And once he had undertaken his own mission, he began to understand how local conditions gradually influenced his ministry. For example, Father Juricich long ago abandoned traditional priestly garb for a simple black kurta worn over pajama pants. He supposed that Rome would be appalled if they knew. But then again, they might not. In the end, it came down to practical concerns: the local clothes were cheap, comfortable, cooler in the heat, and wearing them made him more acceptable to the locals than he would have been had he persisted in western dress.

Among Father Juricich's friends was Daniel Patrick Berrigan. As a young man, Father Juricich fell under the spell of Berrigan's passionate oratory. His philosophy was a variation on the ideology of "faith without works is dead," the *theology of liberation.* "You shall know the truth and the truth shall set you free." What good was it to pray for one's well-being if they were not willing to act—even die—to advance that well-being? What good did it do to offer sacrament to people who were little more than sheep or slaves? Wasn't it freedom of choice that distinguished humankind from the baser creatures? Revisionists like Berrigan interpreted the saints as political activists martyred for their cause.

Coming from Poland, a country betrayed by its allies, divided and conquered, its resistance crushed, his family up the chimneys, the ideology of resistance made sense to Father Juricich—at least when he was young.

It took Father Juricich thirteen arduous years to become a Professed Jesuit. It took him less than two years to land before a defrocking inquest. There had been a scandal, and he had been in the center of it. Retribution was swift and sure. In the spirit of Jesuit liberality, Father Juricich was asked to take a year of reflection to decide what he wanted to do. He went to Poland, but there was nothing left of his home, so he traveled to Jerusalem, thinking that following in the Lord's footsteps might lead him to a clearer understanding. He studied the lives of the early Apostles, especially Thomas and Francis Xavier. Francis Xavier, of the miraculous body—Father Juricich's namesake—was the first to bring the Christian ministry to India. Although he died in China, he was buried in Goa. And that led Father Juricich to India.

It was the miracle of St. Francis Xavier that interested Father Juricich. When Saint Francis Xavier died, to keep his body from being preserved as a relic, a servant poured four bags of lime into the coffin. Several months later, when they checked on the condition of the body, they found it entirely un-decomposed. This was in 1552. His body was transported to Goa—no small feat in the ships of the day—and there Saint Francis Xavier was permanently interred. In 1556 the church dispatched a team of clerics to investigate. They found that the body was "incorruptible" and recommended canonization. This was done in 1622. Theoretically, Francis Xavier's body resisted decomposition down to this day. *Theoretically* because in 1614 Christians from China lopped off St. Francis' right arm and took it back to China. Subsequent relic seekers removed other portions of St. Francis' anatomy, including many of his vital organs. Father Juricich found it disconcerting that the saint could withstand corruption at the hand of nature but was powerless to defend himself against the machinations of the church. But so it was.

Father Juricich requested that he be assigned to the archdiocese in Goa, but his plea was met with disinterest, and he was quietly dispatched to a parish far to the south, in the lonely, neglected, town of Cannanore. At first he didn't mind. Father Juricich relished the opportunity to renew his faith, and he rolled up his sleeves and went to work. But he quickly learned that India had been getting on quite nicely without his interference for seven thousand years and might continue another seven thousand years without noticing he had ever been there. And the town itself, though it had a priest and a good number of Roman Catholic families, was predominately Orthodox Syrian Catholic. Though they welcomed the opportunity Father Juricich represented to attract western charity to Cannanore, besides this, they had little use for him. If he had any illusions about bringing light to the heathen, those hopes died a quick and painless death. So far as he knew, in thirty-eight years of service, Father Juricich had not redeemed a single soul. And now he stood at Rahul Nair's deathbed, and Rahul Nair asked him for a miracle.

* * * * *

Father Juricich leaned forward and grasped Rahul's hand. The priest's hearing was failing with age, and Rahul's broken English, spoken with a thick Malayalam accent, was almost impossible for him to understand, even before the stroke slurred Rahul's speech. "What was that again?" Father Juricich asked.

"He is asking you for a miracle," Naresh said, and the old man nodded.

Father Juricich patted the old man's hands consolingly. "Miracles," he said, "happen by the grace of God. One can ask, but it is more important that one accept in one's heart that God's will, however mysterious, must be obeyed."

*****

Obeyed, Father Juricich thought. One could almost examine life more accurately in the long list of commandments *not* obeyed.

138

There was one original commandment: the fruit of the tree of the knowledge of good and evil, which was *not* to be eaten. From the beginning it was decided that man should not decide what he was or was not to do. And what was man but a patchwork of nerves and instincts and impulses constantly at cross-purposes with our spiritual instructions; for example: Thou shalt not covet thy neighbor's wife.

From the first command came Ten Commandments, from ten a host of proscribed laws governing every conceivable human behavior. And from these myriad of laws came the single Son of Man saying "Love is the Law's fulfillment." So now there was something higher than law, but less specific, more open to interpretation, and it seemed to Father Juricich that the older he got, the less certain he was about anything.

Rahul mumbled something Father Juricich could not hear. He looked at Naresh, who said, "He wants you to take him to visit my brother in America."

Father Juricich almost fell out of his chair. "He wants *what?*"

* * * * *

At home Father Juricich found Shunita busy in the kitchen. When he came in she turned without speaking and pulled a chair back from the table. He sat down—he had long ago given up arguing with Shunita about domestic matters—and she poured him a cup of coffee, then served him rice and vegetable korma with a small bowl of fish curry on the side and some fresh iddly (rice cakes) for him to blot up the gravy. He ate with his fingers, then washed his hands and retired to his room to think.

When it was dark Father Juricich came back into the kitchen. Shunita was curled up asleep on a mat in the corner, but she had left coffee in a pan on the stove. He warmed it and drank, feeling the whole time that she was awake and watching him. When he had finished, he took his walking stick and set out on his nightly rounds.

It had taken Father Juricich years to find his calling (if, in fact, he had a calling). It began with the doubts that gnawed at his faith and manifested themselves in chronic insomnia.

There were six hundred Catholic families in Cannanore when Father Juricich arrived, all of whom could trace their practice back to the Portuguese colonization. He had served in Cannanore for thirty-eight years, and there were still six hundred families, the births offset by deaths, migration to the big cities, or immigration to other countries. This in a town of a million people. The daughters married into other Catholic families, usually from out-of-town, and moved away. The sons married the daughters of other Catholic families, usually from out-of-town, and moved them into their family homes.

When it came down to it, if one wasn't careful, you might confuse Indian Catholics with Hindus. They placed objects of devotion by their front door and images at strategic points in the house. They decorated those images with orange flowers, burned candles and incense, and built small shrines in their yards that looked exactly like Hindu stupas. And despite the church's dire warnings about "godless communism," most of the locals ignored the Papal edict and voted communist anyway.

Father Juricich gradually, grudgingly, gave up the idea that he could change the locals (for better or worse) in any significant way. Over time, he gave up on the notion that religion—any religion—made the slightest difference in people's lives. He wrote letters requesting transfers to other districts, offered in support of his requests that he was ineffective, even threatened to quit the priesthood, all for naught. No replacement was forthcoming. Then the insomnia set in, and to cure the insomnia, his nightly walks.

He was passing through the main bazaar at two in the morning when he came across two men cleaning out sewer pipes. They raked through the muck with their bare hands looking for coins or whatever else of value might turn up.

It was an especially dark night, and Father Juricich watched the two men with a kind of morbid fascination. The monsoons were ending, there was a strong sea breeze blowing, and a thinning canopy of clouds raced by overhead. Suddenly the moon burst through the clouds, and Father Juricich saw that the man closest to him was horribly deformed—his skin from head to toe a massive eruption of what looked like beads, clustered together so tightly that he barely looked human. His companion, too, was deformed, but in a different way. Leprosy had eaten away most of his hands and feet; his nose, lips, and ears. As soon as they saw Father Juricich, they shrank back, but Father Juricich raised his hands and said, in broken Malayalam, "Wait."

He carried a small backpack with a bottle of water and a light meal he intended to eat later on, but instead, he offered the food to the men. They shook their heads, but eventually Father Juricich persuaded them. After, Father Juricich produced two oranges from his bag, peeling them and insisting that the two men eat these also. He asked their names. Thennala and Kandoth, they replied. Their stories were identical. They came from poor villages in the mountains, both stricken as children. Their families could not afford to care for them, so the boys came to the city to beg. But as their diseases progressed, they became so ugly that they could not survive even by begging. They began to sleep days and prowl nights, eking out a living on what they could scavenge from garbage piles and sewer lines.

"Where do you sleep?" Father Juricich asked.

They led him through the bazaar to a slot between two old buildings where a gap less than a foot wide formed a narrow alley. Father Juricich squeezed into the space and followed them down the side and around the rear of one building to a small, closet-sized open space where they had built a tent of plastic sheeting over a narrow platform upon which they shared a single filthy mattress. The owner of the building, Thennala explained, allowed them to stay there in exchange for their picking up the trash and sweeping the sidewalk in front of the building.

Sitting on the mattress was a small, malnourished boy, dressed only in underpants, staring into space. Kandoth had saved half of his orange, and he placed it in the boy's hand. The boy did not acknowledge him, but after holding the orange for a moment, he ate it.

In the dim light, Father Juricich saw Kandoth kneeling in front of the boy. If Kandoth had had lips, Father Juricich thought they would have been parted in a tender smile.

"He is mute," Thennala said, nodding at the boy. "Like an animal."

This was how it began.

The following night Father Juricich took Thennala and Kandoth and the boy rice and iddly left over from his own dinner. He came again a few nights later bringing clothes and sandals. After a week of regular visits, Thennala told the priest about another homeless man, a legless beggar who lived in a culvert under the highway. And then there were two children who turned up, orphans, apparently, one perhaps five, the other two. The younger boy's legs were backwards

141

from birth; he would never walk. And then they came out of the woodwork, the lepers, the crippled, the blind, the sick, the lame, the insane. Within six months Father Juricich was making regular rounds, dispensing food and medicine, clothing, tarps and bedding, sometimes talking, sometimes listening. He visited ruined buildings and culverts under the railroad tracks, bridges, patches of woods, and caves hollowed out by the sea. He learned his way through the maze of drainage ditches, the open sewers that carried away the runoff from the monsoon and the waste from the houses, to find the hidden spots where the deformed passed their nights—or days—undisturbed.

They ate from garbage cans in the alleys behind restaurants. They wrenched spoiled fish from stray cats in the city market, slipping into town in the middle of the night. Some were outwardly deformed, limbs withered from disease, or defective, missing from birth. They were syphilitic. They were blind from herpes. They had been burned and mutilated. And there were others, too, like the boy, not outwardly damaged, but speechless, or psychotic, schizophrenic. Ten years Father Juricich lived in Cannanore, and he had never seen any of these people. In six months he knew more than a hundred by name.

At first, he fed them from his own kitchen, or rather, a grumbling Shunita fed them. She cooked; Father Juricich made the rounds. And when there were more to feed than Father Juricich could reach in a night, Thennala and Kandoth began helping him. He wrote to the archdiocese in Goa asking for money for a kitchen and a car, but they replied that he would have to find funds from the local community. He approached the local church committee but was rebuffed. He tried the communist party office and presented his case as a cause for equality. They listened to his overture sympathetically. Party workers were dispatched to local unions with letters asking for donations, and Father Juricich received some clothes and sandals, a pittance of rice from the rice-growers' cooperative, and a small allowance of fish from the fisherman's cooperative. But over time an ideological split developed in the party, and many members came to resent a supposedly western institution begging off them. "Who are these people?" they asked, meaning the deformed. "Let them approach us directly." A committee was set up to care for the homeless. It fizzled in less than a year.

Around that time, Thendalla and Kandoth led Father Juricich to the edge of town, where crouched in a railway culvert he found the most hideous human being he had met—a woman, perhaps thirty years old, emaciated from malnutrition and shivering from malaria. But the extent of her deformity was almost beyond description. The whole right side of her face was swollen into a ghastly, demonic apparition. Her nose extended nearly a foot, a protuberance that looked more like the trunk of a young elephant than anything human. She was hunchbacked, too, and her right arm had been broken and healed unset so that it was no longer functional. She huddled against the wall, wearing the remains of a burlap sack fashioned into a crude dress.

"How long has she been like this?" Father Juricich asked.

Thendalla shrugged his shoulders. "We only heard about her last night. Some children saw her and thought she was dead."

"She will be if we don't get her to a hospital."

Father Juricich reached for the woman but she recoiled and hissed at him like a snake. "Tell her I won't hurt her," he said.

Thendalla said something in Malayalam, but the woman did not respond. Kandoth tried some broken Hindi, but the woman gave no sign of recognition. Eventually, Kandoth was dispatched to the Syrian-Christian hospital fetch an ambulance, and it arrived near dawn. The woman was wrestled down, strapped to a stretcher, and carted away howling like a dog.

The following afternoon Father Juricich visited her. The staff had placed her in a private ward because they knew the other patients would riot rather than share a room with her. She was heavily sedated.

"Has anyone spoken to her?" he asked.

The nurse replied that they had tried a half-dozen languages, but she had responded to none of them.

For two weeks Father Juricich visited the woman every afternoon bringing her bits of banana and pineapple and milk peda to supplement her hospital diet. She gained weight and strength; antibiotics checked the malaria. But day after day, when Father Juricich visited, he found the woman with her face to the wall.

He wrote letters to state officials inquiring about missing women. They replied that there were thousands of missing women in India, and no official means of keeping track of them. In fact, no one wanted to keep track of them. It was hard enough to place healthy, beautiful girls with husbands without having to worry about the crazy or deformed. They were sorry to hear about her troubles. She was lucky someone hadn't burned or drowned her.

Father Juricich got his temper up over this, and he began writing letters, not just to the archdiocese in Goa, but back to Rome. He wrote international women's organizations, the UN, the Dalai Lama. He wrote the American President, Jimmy Carter, thinking surely he would listen. In reply he received a request for campaign donations and an autographed photo.

* * * * *

One morning a Tibetan monk called at his door. He had read about the priest in Kerala who worked with deformed beggars and traveled from Katmandu to meet him. Father Juricich was stunned; he wasn't aware that anyone had taken note of his work. But the monk produced an article cut from the *Kathmandu Times* about Father Juricich and his letter writing campaign. The monk asked Father Juricich if he could accompany him that night as he made his rounds. Together they visited the culvert where the "elephant woman"—finally discharged from the hospital—made her home.

The woman had a small pile of cow dung smoldering, not that it was cold, but because the smoke kept the mosquitoes at bay. The priest offered her biryani wrapped in a torn page of newspaper. She squatted on her haunches and ate with her fingers.

The monk squatted down opposite her and waited. When she had finished eating, he said something in Tibetan. She froze. He repeated the phrase, and her eyes widened. The monk smiled, said something that was obviously a question, and the woman nodded, then burst into tears. She fell the ground, curled up into a ball, covered her face and rolled away from them; Father Juricich held her until she stopped sobbing. After she composed herself, the monk squatted beside her, and they talked.

This was her story: She was likely born in Tibet and taken to Nepal when she was an infant. She remembered a room in a city, perhaps Kathmandu, and there were other families there, with children, and they slept in the same room, huddled together to stay warm. Later on they moved, probably to India. She described another city, perhaps Mumbai. It was hot. She remembered mosquitoes. It might have been Mumbai, but it might have been Calcutta, or Delhi, as they all have colonies of Tibetan refugees.

She had been diseased from infancy. Her mother cared for her but kept her swathed in blankets to hide her face. She remembered her father but for some reason he left the family. The monk suggested it was to work, Tibetan men often sought work overseas. Apparently he never came back. The mother took the child on a train. The girl was too young to know where they were, but it must have been north; she remembered it was cold. The mother took sick and died, suddenly, there on the train. She remembered there was a commotion, people shouting; she was frightened. She wandered away, unnoticed in the crowd, got off the train—she didn't know where.

She lived for a while in a rail yard, sleeping in empty boxcars. A man used to share his food with her. She looked forward to his company; he was kind. She must have been ten or eleven when a gang of teenage boys came along one night and raped her. They made her keep the blanket wrapped around her face while they did it. When they were finished they wrapped her in the blanket and took her away in the trunk of a car. They stopped, took her out, and then she was falling. They threw her off a bridge into a river. She hit the abutment and fractured her arm—that was how it came to be useless.

How long ago was this? She shrugged her shoulders. Who knows? She crawled out of the river and hid in the woods until hunger and pain drove her to seek help. In a small village she was taken to a doctor. He immobilized her arm without setting the bone and gave her some pills to fight infection. In a day or so the clinic turned her out onto the streets, and she began following the railroad tracks south, living off the garbage people threw from the train. Years passed. She spoke to no one. One day she came to this place, but she was very sick. Now she called it home.

The monk asked if she had a name. The woman shook her head. Was there something she wanted to be called? No response.

Father Juricich patted the woman gently on the shoulder. "I shall call you Sofia," he said, "after my mother."

The following morning the monk left. He promised to take the priest's cause up with the Dalai Lama. Six months passed and Father Juricich heard nothing. He wrote the Dalai Lama. In reply he received an autographed photo.

This, Father Juricich reflected, was not the kind of success that inspired faith. Taking a deep breath he drew upon the lessons he had learned as disciple of Father Berrigan: "Make yourself the crossroad where your enemies collide." He wrote a letter to the local communist party accusing them of showing no more compassion than the western capitalist dogs. He wrote a letter to the Secretary of State of the United States saying that the communists were winning in India because the west stood by and did nothing to alleviate the suffering of the masses. He wrote a letter to the Pope claiming that his neglect was driving the flock into the hands of the communists or the fold of the Muslims. He wrote the United Nations accusing them of practicing "pretty" charity: offering aid where photos of beautiful children exuding charm and gratitude could be used to make the bureaucracy look good while neglecting those most desperately in need.

The first delegation to arrive was from the local communist party, headed by Naresh Nair. He asked, with obvious distaste, what they could do. "I want you to organize the deformed into their own cooperative. They provide you with a valuable service. You will provide them with the means to support themselves with dignity."

The members of the delegation looked at each other and scratched their heads. "What service do these beggars perform?" Naresh asked.

Father Juricich had acquired the Indian habit of talking with his hands, and he gestured emphatically at every point. "They pick up your garbage and unclog your sewers. They perform the most necessary and menial tasks of decent civilization, and you have not the compassion even to feed or clothe them properly. Put out garbage cans, and let them clean the streets at night. Give them tools and brooms so that they can work efficiently. Give them a wage, or at least, let them eat the leftovers from your restaurants. Find someone to make them decent clothes. They might be deformed, but they don't have to be indecent." The cooperative was formed, and most of Father Juricich's demands were met.

The Nair family was, in Indian terms, prosperous. They owned several restaurants, a small tourist hotel, a printing business, and a dozen or so three-wheel autorickshaws that they hired out to cabbies for a daily fee. Rahul in particular seemed irked by Father Juricich's request for aid, but being a practical man he took the lead and pressed the local Lion's and Rotary Clubs to support the priest. Following his lead, many local restaurants began to leave their leftovers in crates behind the back doors. In return, they found their sidewalks swept and windows washed in the morning. Nair himself hired out several deformed workers to work nights. One cleaned his autorickshaws. Another he taught to operate the printing press at night when he had large or rush orders.

A few months later a delegation arrived from New Delhi asking what they could do for the "hidden homeless" on a national scale. Two officials were assigned to follow Father Juricich around for a week and calculate what percentage of the local population might be homeless and in need and not registered with the census. They left, and a few months later Father Juricich received a letter advising him that one of the local hospitals had been budgeted a small amount to care for the mentally ill.

A similar letter arrived from the United Nations. They would send a team to study Father Juricich's ministry and see what could be learned so that these people could be helped on an international scale. The representatives spent a week in Cannanore, then departed. A few months later the U.N. proposed, through the World Health Organization, to initiate a grass roots campaign to identify and provide basic services for the poorest of the poor. They cited Mother Teresa as a role model.

The United States earmarked money for the relief of the poor, as well, though these funds were pillaged so thoroughly by corrupt officials at the national and state levels that, as far as Father Juricich could tell, not a rupee ever made it to the needy.

Finally, Father Juricich received a letter advising him that a delegation from Rome would be dispatched to see him, and for the first time in his career as a priest, he was proud. The local families banded together to paint the church and prepare a welcome feast. They served spiced fish steamed in banana leaves with saffron rice and vegetable masala. The delegates smiled and led mass and offered special prayers and made glowing pronouncements about the little community that could. Afterwards, in private, they warned Father Juricich that he had been sent to Cannanore as punishment and if he knew what was good for him he would keep a low profile. There were still those who did not like to be reminded of his presence. When they left, he sank into a deep depression.

* * * * *

Twenty years passed. Father Juricich, walking in the dark, stepped in a hole and fell. He broke his right leg so badly he could not extract himself and lay in the middle of the road until workers found him in the morning. His first recollection was being lifted by many hands and gently placed on a stretcher. Surgeons from the Orthodox-Syrian hospital set the bone. They gave him a private room for his recovery. After that, he took to walking with a cane, not so much because he needed it to stand, but because, like a blind man, he could feel the road ahead of his step.

As Father Juricich approached his eightieth birthday, his nightly rounds felt more like visiting old friends. He no longer needed to distribute meals, though he carried a pocketful of milk peda candies to share with homeless children. He also dispensed antibiotics and other medicines, as needed, to those still reluctant to come in to town for assistance.

Thenalla and Sofia remained his closest friends. Kandoth had died some years back, but Thenalla still plugged on, living squeezed like a cockroach in the same crack between the same buildings. He had, for a time, been elected a representative to the state government under the rules requiring representation by the lower castes but had found politics difficult and felt the public display of his handicap actually worked against the needs of the poor. Sofia had moved closer to town and lived a squatter's hut she built on the fenced grounds surrounding an electrical transformer. She had learned enough Malayalam to get by, and often came to visit Father Juricich in his home, arriving in the late afternoon when she knew he would be getting ready for his rounds. She still swathed her face in a shawl, and in the dark she almost passed for a Muslim with only her eyes and nose visible through the veil.

* * * * *

Father Juricich slept fitfully, waking every few hours from dreams that were sometimes rhapsodic, and other times disturbingly sexual. He woke shortly before noon, performed his devotional, eeked out a sparse breakfast under Shunita's critical eye, and set out to check on Rahul Nair.

The Nair compound was slightly less crowded though there were still a number of relatives camped out downstairs and in the hall. Upstairs, Mrs. Nair, looking pale, sat on the edge of the bed but stood

148

to one side when Father Juricich arrived. The old man looked like he hadn't moved.

"Tell me," Father Juricich said, pulling a chair close to the bed, "why do you want to go to America?"

Rahul spoke slowly, laboriously churning out the words. "I want to visit my son."

"Why do you want me to take you?"

"I have no money."

"What do you mean? Why, you are one of the wealthiest men in town!"

"This is not so. I have divided a little for all of my sons and grandsons, but for myself, there is nothing. I will die soon. I must visit my son."

"But the Nair fortune . . . "

"There is no fortune. We have been living on reputation. What I had was sufficient for myself, but divided among my sons . . . "

The priest rested his elbow on his knee and his chin in his hand. "But your son in America . . ."

"He has supported us with a portion of his income for years. It was his duty to his family. But he and I have a disagreement going back many years. He will not come here. He will not send for me. I must go to him. It is the only way."

"What happened between you?"

"There are two things, priest," Rahul said. "And if I tell you, you must repeat this to no one. It must be as though we never spoke."

"All right."

"The first was that many years ago, I suspected my wife of adultery. It was probably just foolish jealousy on my part, but it might have happened. Over the years, it gave me pause to question whether Venkadath was really mine. I favored Naresh. Venkadath's mother favored him. Perhaps it was this division that forced him to leave. He wanted to go to America. I did not care if he stayed. But when he married an American girl, a Christian, and when he became a Christian himself, I told him that he was no longer my son—if he ever was."

"And now?"

"We are old, priest, and many things change. A young man sees everything and knows nothing because he has no perspective from which to understand. An old man sees nothing and knows everything because everything he sees reminds him of something else that was. I know much now that I did not see then. Have you read Khalil Gibran?"

"Yes."

"Then you know that children may be given us, but they are never really ours. I failed my son, and now I want only to give him back

149

the thing I took from him, the respect of his father. He will not come to me, priest, I must go to him. And I am poor but no longer too proud to ask. I have not time for the luxury of pride. You will help me, yes?"

"Rahul. I would do anything to help you, but I am a poor priest myself. I have taken a vow of poverty regarding the things of this world. I have only a small pension from the church, a home, a few clothes. What would you have me do?"

"With all of the power at your command, is there no one you can write? No authority you can draw on?"

"It would take a miracle for me to find enough money to send you to America. And you are not well, how would you withstand the rigors of the journey?"

"For how many years you have preached that, "With God, anything is possible." Now you say that it will take a miracle? Show me the miracle. I can make the journey priest. If you can provide the money, I will join into your church. I will convert and become a Christian. Just help me to go and see my son one last time before I die."

"Do you mean this?" Father Juricich asked. "Do you know what this means?"

"I do and I do," Rahul replied.

Father Juricich limped home, his leg aching for no apparent reason. In Europe people claimed that aching bones meant a change in the weather. In Kerala there were two summers and two monsoons—not much change to ache over.

Shunita had marinated a chicken and roasted it on a skewer. It was one of Father Juricich's favorite dishes. With it she served rice and vegetables steamed together in a banana leaf with bay leaves and cloves. Sofia was there, too, sitting in a corner when he arrived.

Father Juricich paused only to wash his face and hands, then joined them in the kitchen. He picked at his food. Lately, even his favorite meals did not arouse his interest, and Shunita scolded him for not eating. She made him lime tea. Sofia went out and returned an hour later with Thennala. He brought some cake. "The bakery left it for me," he explained.

"I'm just tired," Father Juricich said. "I haven't been sleeping well."

"What is happening with old man Nair?" Thennala asked.

"It is quite absurd, really. He wants me to send him to America."

"To America? Why? Are there not doctors enough here?"

"It is about his son, not his condition."

"His son is also a doctor?"

"A dentist, but that is not the reason. I really can't say any more about it. I promised."

"Why would he ask you?"

"He thinks that I can help, foolish old man." Father Juricich grimaced and rubbed his forehead with his right hand. "He says he'll convert to Catholicism if I can send him to America."

"Convert? You must be joking."

"I would never joke about a thing like that."

* * * * *

That night, lying in bed, Father Juricich pondered the intricacies of Indian familial life. Men could have, or used to have, second wives, though the laws had changed about that recently. And they often had girlfriends they kept with the full knowledge of their wives. Wives might not approve of the arrangement, but there was little they could do about it. Once divorced, Indian women almost never remarried. Once separated, they might be kept in their birth home, but they might be thrown out into the streets to fend for themselves, too. On the other hand, women caught at adultery could be stoned, even burned alive. The double standard was perplexing, but not entirely unlike western culture. Only in the past thirty years had women begun to acquire something like gender equality in the west, and even this was a dubious blessing. Everything was topsy-turvy; nobody knew their place anymore. The turmoil in the church merely reflected the turmoil in society: openly homosexual priests, women clamoring for ordination, disillusioned members seeking God through alternative channels. Who knew what the future held? Father Juricich was seventy-nine years old and no mention had been made of his retiring, no replacement groomed, or even, as far as he knew, planned for the Cannanore district.

When he arrived in Cannanore, Father Juricich suggested that the Church host traditional morning mass, a six o'clock, ten o'clock, and noon. The local priest told him to go ahead if he wanted. What Father Juricich found was that in Kerala, people didn't stir from their homes until ten. They spent the cool morning hours sleeping or tending to domestic affairs. The six o'clock mass failed in the first week—not a single parishioner showed. He cancelled the ten o'clock within a month, and the noon by the end of his first year. The flock had met once a week on Sundays, probably since St. Francis himself preached to them. One energetic priest was not going to turn the tide of five hundred years of tradition. And if Father Juricich couldn't affect even a small flock of supposedly faithful followers, what chance did he have to work a miracle for a non-believer? By what right did he even ask? Rahul was partly right, Father Juricich thought. A young man saw everything and knew nothing. An old man saw nothing and knew . . . nothing?

That night, instead of making his usual rounds, Father Juricich rested in his room. He fell asleep in the early hours of the morning and dreamed of Tunisia. He recalled, in his dream, seeing General Montgomery pass by in his staff car early one morning, resplendent in a crisp uniform with a black scarf and a red beret. Then-corporal Juricich saluted, and the general acknowledged the salute by waving his riding crop. And Father Juricich remembered the seemingly endless moment of paralytic fear when his truck struck the mine and he was lifted up and thrown (as he later described it) "ass over teakettle." And he remembered the shock of the troop ship being struck by the torpedo. Father Juricich had been on deck late—another of his insomniac nights, and the force of the explosion hurled him into the water. His first fear had been that he had re-injured his back, but though he felt the grate of bone on bone, he could still swim enough to stay afloat until a rescue ship caught him in its spotlight. But for a few terrifying moments he was utterly alone in the waters of the North Atlantic, and it was cold, and he wondered about his family, and whether his mother had really done him a favor whisking him out of Poland ahead of the invasion. Nothing he had experienced since that moment, alone in the North Atlantic, had challenged his realization that a man was a very insignificant thing compared to the universe. But in that moment, floating numb in the freezing water, Father Juricich knew with certainty that he was not going to die, and that having dodged death's hammer-stroke twice, God must have something greater in store for him, and that was the spark of faith that kept him going. And now, sixty years later, Father Francis Xavier Juricich could not say what that greater thing was, and for the first time in years, he wept.

In the morning he emerged from his room ashen and refused anything but tea. He retired to the church where he prayed alone, and, embarrassingly, fell asleep in the front pew. Thenalla woke him, gently shaking the priest's shoulder.

"How much," he asked, "is a ticket to America?"

Father Juricich was confused. "What," he replied, "is everyone going to America now?"

"No, I only wondered."

"I don't know, but it must be many lakhs of rupees. Ask Suliman, the travel agent. He would know."

That evening Father Juricich felt somewhat refreshed and ate more than he had in several days. But afterwards his stomach cramped, and he took to bed.

In the morning, Shunita summoned a doctor. He listened to Father Juricich's rumbling bowels through a cold stethoscope and then proscribed a combination of antibiotics and Ayurvedic medication. Thenalla came to visit in the afternoon, and Sofia in the evening. The following day was Sunday, and Father Juricich was well enough to lead mass, though he shortened his sermon to only a few words, citing his poor health as an excuse. No one complained.

After the service, he was met outside by Thennala, who asked Father Juricich how much money he could contribute towards a ticket for Rahul Nair. Thennala had inquired of the travel agent, but the physician said it was impossible for Rahul to travel alone, and that if he were to make the trip at all, a nurse would have to be in constant attendance.

"Are you gone mad?" Father Juricich asked.

Thennala shook his head.

Father Juricich had set aside a small portion of his pension for emergencies. "I suppose," he said, "if it came down to it, I could contribute five or ten thousand rupees."

Thennala burst into a radiant smile. "Then it is done," he replied.

"What?" Father Juricich gasped. "How?"

"We all chipped in," Thennala said. "Every one his portion. You have done much for us, it was time we did something for you."

* * * * *

Rahul Nair and his nurse left for America—Minneapolis—on a Thursday morning. A large delegation turned out at the airport to see them off. Father Juricich, still bothered by his stomach, turned out also, leaning heavily on his staff. Afterwards, and for the first time in weeks, he slept soundly and was not disturbed by dreams. He awoke around three, dined with Shunita, and left near seven for his nightly rounds. Thenalla found him the next morning unconscious by the side of the road. On his eightieth birthday, Father Juricich had been struck by a car.

Ruhal Nair suffered another stroke on the plane on the way home from America and died 36,000 feet over the Pacific Ocean. Father Juricich received the new stoically, lying in his hospital bed. Unless there was some private pact between Rahul and God, it seemed Father Juricich would die with his perfect record of evangelistic ineptitude intact. Perhaps, he wondered, they will name an order after me, someday—The Juricichians—dedicated to burying their heads in the sand and converting no one. It would be an easy order to join. Or would it?

That night Father Juricich dreamed of Poland, and of the long train ride that carried him to France, and then of the ship that took him to Scotland, and the distant relatives who met him on the pier when he arrived. But the dream was confusing, for Scotland was hot and covered with palm trees, and the Atlantic was flat and calm, and among the relatives were dozens of friends and co-workers whom Father Juricich had known much later in life, and Father Juricich was so tired that when he arrived that he could hardly walk down the gangway.

Shunita found him in the morning when he failed to rise for his coffee. Father Juricich died in his sleep. By nightfall, the little cottage behind the church was awash in a sea of lighted candles. Notes arrived from Muslims and Hindus; even the local communist party chief placed a wreath in the front yard. From as far away as Calcutta the blind and the lame and sick and the deformed came to pay their respects—thousands upon thousands, walking in the daylight to reach Cannanore. Father Juricich had left a will. In his own typically headstrong fashion, he requested that his body be cremated.

* * * * *

Two months later a replacement priest arrived from Goa. The new priest settled into the cottage, Shunita cooked and cleaned for him, but the new priest made no effort, as Father Juricich had, to walk the streets at night. One morning, over coffee, he asked Shunita who was with Father Juricich after he died, and if it was true, what was whispered about him.

"What do they whisper?" Shunita asked.

"They say that a long time ago, when Father Juricich was in Ireland, he was involved in a scandal with a married woman, a Protestant, at that. They were found out, and someone—who knows who—took him and the woman away. They killed the woman, but the priest, according to rumor, was castrated. Cut off his penis, too. I just wondered if, when they washed the body, and I suppose someone must have washed the body, if anyone saw anything . . . unusual."

Shunita considered the question for a moment. What she remembered the most about that day was that when Sofia heard the news, she had rushed to the cottage and threw herself on the priest's body. She could be neither torn from that embrace, nor consoled. Shunita refilled the priest's cup. "No," she said, shaking her head for emphasis, "he was perfect."